MR. MAY

HEROES OF ROGUE VALLEY: CALENDAR
GUYS
BOOK 5

ANN ROTH

Published by Oliver-Heber Books

0 9 8 7 6 5 4 3 2 1

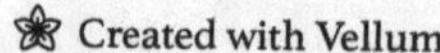 Created with Vellum

INTRODUCTION

Welcome to Ann Roth's exciting new series, Heroes of Rogue Valley: Calendar Guys series. Twelve months, 12 gorgeous firefighter heroes and the women who steal into their hearts and forever change their lives.

Meet Mr. May:

Firefighter Hank Gardener harbors a heavy secret and crushing guilt —he failed to contain the fire that gutted Deanna Oliver's home and damaged the bed & breakfast she is painstakingly renovating. Can he atone for his mistake and help her rebuild out of the ashes, or will his secret destroy them both?

Mr. May–Hank Gardner
    Age 30, 6'1" tall, 184 pounds
    Single
    Proud Junior Firefighter
    Time with Guff's Lake Fire Department: 4 years

1

For the first time in almost a year Deanna Oliver felt like her old self—determined and ready to make her dream a reality. Her mind spinning with ideas, she exited the General Hardware parking lot and turned toward home. An almost twenty-mile round-trip drive, but the class she'd taken for do-it-yourself remodelers this morning had been worth the time.

Patching walls, priming and painting—she had those down now. She also had names of reputable experts, people far more knowledgeable than Rusty, to help renovate the B&B, aka Oliver's Bed & Breakfast.

Who needed him, anyway? She could and would do this alone. Deanna raised her chin. Unlike her mother, she refused to turn a blind eye on a man who lied and cheated—nor was she going to leave Guff's Lake. This was home and always would be.

Horn blaring, siren screaming, and lights flashing, a fire truck some distance behind her warned vehicles out of its way. Deanna pulled her hatchback onto the shoulder of Kirkdale Road. Somehow when she hadn't been looking fall had crept up. The fields and trees in the Rogue Valley had responded with their usual array of autumn colors, brightening the otherwise gray morning.

The truck roared past. Another soon followed. A fire requiring two trucks must be a bad one. Feeling for the poor family or business owner involved, Deanna shook her head. Once the vehicles barreled by and passed out of view, she returned to her thoughts.

The down payment on the property and additional costs of fixing up the bungalow adjacent to the bed & breakfast so that she and Rusty could move in had all but emptied her savings account. In the year since he'd left, thanks to careful budgeting and her two jobs at the Guff's Lake Resort Hotel, she'd replenished it enough to continue with the renovations.

By nature impatient, she preferred immediate results for her efforts. But making her dream into reality? For that she had abundant patience. As long as she moved forward, slow, steady progress would do.

She'd already decided on a color palette—soft, soothing colors for the bedrooms, bright, cheerful colors for the bathrooms, the glistening warmth of the natural wood wainscoting for the living and dining rooms, and for the stairs leading to the second floor. Faux oriental rugs over the wood and new carpeting in the bedrooms would add a homey touch and mute footsteps, with new lighting to further enhance the feeling of comfort and welcome.

She would use the rest of today and all day tomorrow, her days off, to line up bids for installing drywall and, even if she didn't have the funds yet, for refinishing the wood floors and the risers. Maybe she'd check out carpeting for the bedrooms.

The exit for Guff's Lake Resort was just ahead.

Deanna's property lay five miles south of the resort, which made commuting quick and easy.

She signaled and headed toward the lake, which lay nestled in the foothills of the Siskiyou Mountains. Despite the thick clouds obscuring the snow-dusted peaks of the majestic mountains, they and four-mile diameter lake made for a spectacular view she never tired of.

The siren's howl again interrupted her thoughts, growing louder by the second before it abruptly stopped. Where was it coming from?

Not the resort, she hoped. She pulled into the parking area and drove slowly around the premises. To her relief, everything looked normal.

Then where? Alert and seeking the source of whatever had summoned the two fire trucks, she cracked the window open and continued toward home. No scent of smoke or signs of a fire anywhere—until she approached Ridge Road, where she lived.

There it was, the ominous smoke she'd sought out. It shrouded the windshield and all but obscured any visibility. Deanna slowed to a crawl. The acrid smell filled her nostrils.

A sudden gust of wind cleared the air and she could see again. The smoke seemed to be coming from her neighborhood.

Oh, no. Please don't let it be Bea's place. Her elderly friend lived on a fixed income and was in no shape to deal with a fire.

Sick with dread, Deanna drove the last few miles to Ridge Road. Bea and a handful of neighbors had gathered around the fire trucks, one parked on the street and the other in the driveway at Deanna's house —what was left of it.

The tiny bungalow she'd called home for the past

fifteen months was a pile of smoking debris that reeked of loss and ruin. The adjacent bed & breakfast still stood, but the side facing the bungalow had been damaged.

With a mounting sense of horror, Deanna jumped out of the car and dashed forward.

~

HANK GARDENER WAS COILING hose when a hatchback screeched to a halt in the middle of the road. The woman who exited and flew toward him looked to be in her mid-twenties. In her haste her open trench coat flapped wide at her sides, revealing a willowy body.

She raced right past him—or would have if he hadn't snagged her by the arm. "Stay back, ma'am."

Barely reaching his shoulder, she stiffened, her eyes wide with shock. "But that's my house. Or was."

She buried her head in her hands, locks of sandy blond hair curtaining her face as if she couldn't bear to see the smoking pile of destruction.

Hank understood. Since joining the Guff's Lake Fire Department four years ago he'd witnessed the pain of similar losses up close and personal many times.

Yet before today he'd never been responsible for the disaster.

Every firefighter worth his salt knew how to read the smoke caused by a fire. The color, speed, and direction spoke volumes and indicated changing fire conditions. Yet he'd misread the warnings.

Scratch that. He hadn't read them at all.

People reacted in different ways. Some seemed shell-shocked, while others collapsed in grief. She looked ready to cry.

Hank wanted to pull her into a comforting embrace. This woman he'd never laid eyes on. He didn't even know her name.

"I'm sorry," he offered. Not much of a consolation, but it'd have to do.

She straightened, nodded, and blinked hard as if damming up the tears. "I made a point of turning off all the baseboard heaters before I left this morning. How did the fire start?"

"We don't know the cause yet. According to your neighbors there were no pets inside."

"That's right. But my clothes and other personal things, records for what I've spent on remodeling Oliver's—the B&B next door—everything except what I'm wearing now, my laptop, and cell phone was in there. Oh, God—Froggy. Please let him be safe."

"You do have a pet," he said.

She shook her head. "Froggy is ceramic and very dear to me. Surely he survived. I have to find him!"

He winced at the bleak devastation on her face, hated that he couldn't go back and redo the last forty minutes. Story of his life. "You can't go near the rubble for at least twenty-four hours," he said. "It's too hot. Plus the claims adjustor will want to look around first. You should call your insurance company right away."

"I will. What do I do now?" she muttered as if to herself. "Where am I going to sleep tonight?"

"Do you have family in the area?"

She shook her head. "I guess I'll ask one of my friends or check in at the hotel."

"Hotel?"

"The one at the Guff's Lake Resort. When can I get into the B&B to assess the damage?"

"It'll be a while yet. First a crewmate and I need to

inspect the premises. We'll let you know if it's safe for you to enter. I need to get back to the job."

"Of course."

After parking her car up the street, she trudged toward the neighbors huddled nearby. They greeted her with sympathetic looks and warm hugs.

Max, Hank's best bud, approached and nodded at the woman. "Who's that?"

"I didn't catch her name. She's the property owner."

"Bummer."

Of the worst kind. And Hank's sorry ass was to blame. His first failure as a firefighter, but face it, he was always screwing up something. Rarely on the job, and never this bad. Sure, back when he'd worked as a full-time paramedic he'd made a few rookie mistakes, but nothing dangerous or harmful. Pretty much everything in his love life, though.

Early on, his parents had pegged him as a major disappointment. Hell, his being born at all had been a major inconvenience. According to them he'd been a surprise and throughout his childhood, he'd often felt like an afterthought. He'd always suspected they'd wanted only one kid—Hudson.

Time and again he'd let them down, until the day he'd shattered any chance of redeeming himself. But he didn't like to think about that.

Then there was Gretchen. Not gonna think about his most recent ex, either. "If I'd been on the ball we could have saved her house and prevented damage to the bed & breakfast," he muttered.

"Hey, you weren't the only one battling that blaze. It was a team effort."

"I was the one with the hose."

"Gus, Tony, and Nate don't count?"

"They were inside. I was out here." Hank's failure to note the changing smoke patterns and density had endangered his teammates and cost precious minutes that could have been used to save the bungalow. He kicked at the ground.

"Cut yourself some slack, man. In all the smoke it was difficult if not impossible to see what was happening. Reduced visibility has always been a bitch. Yeah, it sucks that we lost the house, but the crew is okay and we saved the other structure. Let's grab our gear and inspect that mother."

At the fire truck Hank exchanged the hose and SCBA, or self-contained breathing apparatus, for an infrared device designed to check for undetected heat inside the walls. Max brought other equipment and a clipboard for the inspection report. They headed over.

Five bedrooms and five bathrooms, and the large living and dining rooms made for a perfect bed and breakfast—or would at some point.

Currently, the kitchen floor was stripped down to its studs, and the floors of the living and dining room were scarred up and in need of TLC. On the steps leading upstairs and in the bedrooms, old carpeting lay in piles over fir boards, and a good seventy percent of the walls had been stripped to the studs.

But the structure was sound enough. No discernable fire damage except for the chunks of siding that had been hacked up, two broken windows on the south side of the house, and the pool of water on the floor under the windows.

"I'll give her the structure status," Hank volunteered after they stowed the infrared devices and other equipment in the truck.

Max nodded. "I'll finish writing up the report."

The property owner broke away from her neighbors and moved quickly toward Hank. He hadn't really looked at her before. She was pretty, her stride purposeful, giving her an air of a woman who didn't waste time.

On the way she fiddled with her shoulder-length hair, gathering it into a low ponytail. "Well?" she asked, her expression hopeful.

"The exterior damage is contained to the siding and two main floor windows on the south of the building, plus a fair amount of standing water on the main floor from containing the fire before it spread," he explained. "You'll want to get it off the floor as soon as possible. Your insurance company will know who to call.

"Without furniture, carpeting, or drapes, the interior smoke damage is minimal. A good airing out should take care of it."

She nodded and her shoulders bowed for a moment as if under an invisible weight. "I suppose that's something to be thankful for."

"You lost a great deal this morning," he said, briefly squeezing her shoulder. Through the trench coat he felt her clavicle. She could use some meat on her body. "Have you heard about our benefit fund?"

She nodded. "For people who have lost their homes and other things in a fire. That's why you sell calendars, to raise money for the fund. Shoot, now my copy is gone, too. You're Hank—Mr. May."

The calendar had made him a familiar face and he was used to people recognizing him. "That's me. And you are—"

"Deanna Oliver. I appreciate what you and the other firefighters did today."

Feeling like a fraud for his failings, Hank avoided her gaze. "Nothing will make up for what happened today, but we can help. If your insurance falls short of what you need, and it most always does, go to our website for our online assistance form. Or stop by the station and pick up a hard copy."

"Beyond what the insurance covers, I don't need help." Her chin rose to regal heights. "I've been in bad situations before and I managed all right on my own."

Hank wanted to know more, but her past wasn't his business. Whatever had happened had made her tough and proud, and for what she was dealing with she'd need every ounce of both. "I would, but suit yourself. Did you find a place to stay?"

"Miss Beasley, the short, white-haired woman over there, offered me her couch for a couple nights."

Relieved she had a place to bunk at least temporarily, he nodded. "If you have questions about anything, here's my card." He dug into his pocket and extracted two. "One for you and one for the insurance company."

She dropped both into her purse. "My insurance man said he'd meet me here shortly."

"That's good. Best of luck to you." Hank rejoined his buds and helped pack up the gear.

By then Max had completed the inspection report and handed a copy to Deanna. Just before Liam, the engineer driving the truck, pulled away from the property, thunder boomed and the rain started.

Now the rain comes. Deanna was suffering enough. She didn't need to get drenched and catch cold. If Hank had had an umbrella with him he'd have given it to her. He didn't. She pulled up the hood of her trench coat and hunched up inside it.

As if sensing his scrutiny she raised her hand in a universal sigh of thanks and good-bye. He didn't tear his gaze away until the truck rounded the corner.

2

———————

By lunchtime Monday the rain stopped. Not so with the fire and medic emergencies, which continued through the night and into Tuesday. One call after another, all day long.

After four years of double back-to-back, twenty-four hour shifts, Hank was used to functioning on little sleep. By the time dinner rolled around, he was running on fumes and as hungry as a bear after hibernation.

At eighteen hundred hours sharp he joined the captain and his eleven crewmates at the big table in the firehouse kitchen. This was Daniel's week to cook dinner—Hank had done the honors the previous week—and his spicy chili casserole smelled great. The sides looked good, too.

As the steaming platters of food passed from man to man, Hank's mouth watered. Once every plate had been filled they bent to the task of slaking their hunger. For a while, except for the clink of silverware against dishes, the room was silent.

"Crazy few days, huh?" Max said a few minutes later. "I'd kill for a slow night."

Hank seconded that, but in a town of roughly twenty thousand residents, anything could happen.

Rafe yawned. "We could all do with a solid eight hours' sleep."

"Jillian would appreciate that." Max's mouth quirked. "She's bound to want you active and awake all night."

Good-natured laughs all around, Rafe's loudest of all. Dude was whipped and then some.

"The report from the insurance company on the cause of the fire on Ridge Road just came in," Adam commented.

Hank looked up from his plate. Since the fire at Deanna's place yesterday he'd thought about her a lot. He'd also rehashed his role in making the situation much worse than it should have been. After graduating near the top of his fire science class and with umpteen fires under his belt, he'd assumed he had the art of smoke reading down. Nope, and his failure weighed heavy on his shoulders.

"And?" he asked.

"Old aluminum wiring. That bungalow was using its original fuse box from some fifty years ago."

"No wonder the place caught fire," Rafe commented. "If you ask me, Deanna is an ideal candidate for assistance from the benefit fund. She ought to apply."

Hank swallowed a mouthful of food. "That's what I told her the other day. She claims she isn't interested, but I think I can change her mind."

"It's not your business to do that," Captain Comings reminded him.

"It is when I'm responsible for what happened."

"Here we go again," Adam muttered. "Will you quit beating yourself up? You didn't do anything wrong.

Visibility sucked. Any one of us would have missed the signs."

All the guys started talking at once until the captain's warning growl shut them up. "You have to let this go, Hank," he ordered. "Like Adam said, you did your best—we all did. Learn from this and move on. Otherwise, you'll be required to seek counseling."

Not happening. Hank didn't want that on his record. Besides, he didn't need therapy. "Yes, sir. I could use a refresher on reading smoke."

Regular in-house training on a variety of subjects was a given, and the captain gave an approving nod. "Sounds like a good class for the entire crew." He singled out Max, who'd been with the GLFD thirteen years. "I want you to facilitate that."

The discussion shifted to when and how. Hank listened, offered his twenty-five cents, and then tuned out.

Regardless what the captain said, he meant to convince Deanna to apply for the money she deserved. As yet he didn't know how, but he would make it happen.

"THANKS FOR LETTING me stay here again tonight," Deanna told Bea as she made up the woman's sofa bed Tuesday evening.

Her seventy-something friend smiled. "It's no trouble at all—I enjoy your company. I wish I had an extra bedroom. Then you could stay as long as you like."

"No worries–Vi offered me the futon at her place."

A generous offer from Deanna's bestie—except for several problems, the biggest being that Vi had recently moved in with her boyfriend, Rick. Also, like

Bea, their living quarters had only one bedroom. More than a night or two would put a strain on all three of them.

"After that, I'll stay at the hotel," Deanna added. "With tons of vacancies this time of year, I can get a room at a decent discount."

Still costlier than renting an apartment. She hated wasting the money. Everything spent on a hotel room took funds away from Oliver's, which now, on top of renovations, also needed repairs from the damage it had suffered during the fire.

"I expect to hear from my insurance agent any day now," she finished, crossing her fingers that the reimbursement funds came through fast.

The sooner, the better. Since the fire, her hard-earned savings had again dwindled alarmingly. Hiring someone to suck the water off the B&B's floor hadn't been cheap, although her insurance would eventually cover most of the expense. Recently she'd renewed the policy for a hefty amount that had left her grumbling. As of yesterday she'd changed her tune. Protection in an emergency like hers made the renewal amount worth the price.

But insurance wouldn't cover what she'd spent to replace her makeup and toiletries, socks, underwear, shoes, and clothing. Necessities that added up at lightning speed. Plus there were bills to pay, including the mortgage, which didn't stop even for a disaster.

Forget rebuilding the bungalow. She preferred to put every cent toward Oliver's, starting with new windows and repairs to the siding. Quickly, if possible.

She also needed money for an apartment. No landlord would rent to her without a check upfront covering first and last month rent and a damage deposit.

Bea shook her head. "I don't have much in savings, but I can loan you a little—something to tide you over until you get your check from the insurance company."

"Hey, I'm still working full time. I earn decent wages at the front desk and make good tips at the Hearthstone," she reminded Bea. Customers at the resort's upscale restaurant tended to tip generously.

"But this is the slow season."

"For tourists but not locals. This time of year we do a brisk business with them. Once ski season starts in mid-November, our tourist guests will fill the dining room. So you see, I don't need your money. I'll be fine."

If Deanna said it enough, surely it would be true.

She was beginning to wonder if she'd ever save enough to turn Oliver's into the cozy inn she imagined, let alone open for business.

Slow and steady, she reminded herself.

She couldn't help recalling Hank Gardener's suggestion that she use the firefighter benefit fund. Having grown up with parents who milked any available assistance program for every dime they could get, Deanna preferred to pull herself up by her own bootstraps. She was nobody's charity case.

Still, she appreciated Hank's concern. It'd been a while since a man had cared about her welfare, and he'd made her feel warm inside.

But guys who seemed nice in the beginning often lied. Rusty wasn't the first smooth talker she'd believed when she shouldn't have. He was the latest in a line of ex-boyfriends stretching behind him as far back as middle school. Even her own father had let her down. She was through depending on a man for anything.

"Speaking of eating out, I'm taking you to breakfast tomorrow morning," Deanna told Bea.

Her way of repaying her kind friend for putting her up. Bea lived on a fixed income and didn't go out to eat often.

Behind her bifocals the older woman's brown eyes sparkled. "I'd like that. But didn't you schedule appointments before work to look at apartments?"

"Not until ten, and neither of them is far from here. After breakfast I'll drop you off, then see the apartments. If you and I leave the house around seven forty-five, we should have plenty of time for a leisurely meal. Is that doable, or would you rather sleep in?"

"For breakfast out, I'm happy to get up."

Bea rubbed her hands together, making Deanna laugh. "Where would you like to go?"

"Rosemary's," she replied without hesitation. "I love the food and the Sam's Treats bakery goodies."

"So do I, and I haven't eaten there in ages. This will be a treat for both of us."

"You need that," Bea said. "You lost so much."

Deanna felt like sobbing. Swallowing hard, she held herself together and smiled.

Bea gave her a sympathetic look. "You're a strong one, all right, but you're only human. You lost your home and most of your possessions. It's okay to cry. I know I would."

"I'm afraid that if I do, I may not stop," Deanna admitted. Besides, she prided herself on her strength. Crying showed a person's weakness, and tears were for when she was in the shower, where no one would hear.

"You don't have to worry about that in this house," Bea said. "Lord knows, I cried a whole river when I lost everything."

She meant Richard Carner, her one true love. He'd died long before Deanna had met her friend. Although Bea didn't talk about him often, Deanna had heard the story several times. They'd met when Richard had hired Bea to care for his wife, who suffered from Alzheimer's.

As the poor woman declined mentally and physically over the course of a year, Bea and Richard had fallen in love. After his wife had passed away, they'd set a wedding date. Sadly, before it took place, a heart attack had stolen Richard from Bea.

Deanna doubted she'd ever find a love as true as theirs. She wanted to, but after Rusty and her other failed relationships she no longer trusted her judgment. The men she gravitated toward always turned out to be unreliable.

The problem lay with her heart. Her feelings always got in the way, crowding out levelheadedness and the danger signs any person with common sense would recognize. In that way she was way too much like her mother.

"There's a big difference between what you lost and what I did," she said.

"Loss is loss."

Tired of talking about it, Deanna yawned and stretched. Thanks to the fire she hadn't been able to sleep much. "I'm exhausted," she said. "I'm sure you are, too. We should both get some sleep."

"All right. Good night, Deanna." Bea headed for her room.

Before turning out the light, Deanna checked email on her phone. And a good thing—Matt, her insurance agent, had sent a copy of the insurance report. To her shock, the report showed the cause of the fire to be the old aluminum wiring.

Wait—how could that be? Rusty had updated it. At least he'd said he had.

Stunned, she set the phone facedown, as if hiding the facts could change the truth that he'd lied about this as well as his marital status.

He'd only needed to admit he couldn't do the job. She'd have hired someone and would still be living in the bungalow.

Instead he'd chosen to deceive her.

Was there no end to his duplicity? Feeling naïve and stupid all over again for ever taking him at his word, Deanna wanted to scream. She wanted to slap his lying face.

"Never again," she swore aloud.

The tears came at last. She muffled them with her pillow. After a while, worn out, she finished reading the report. Apparently the insurance company still planned to reimburse her. Matt promised to call Friday morning.

She blew out a relieved breath, flipped out the light, burrowed under the covers, and waited for the oblivion of sleep.

But every time she closed her eyes she saw the rubble that had once been her home. After spending hours combing through the remains and looking for her possessions this afternoon, she'd found a few charred pots and pans, several wire hangers, and a few melted forks—nothing of value.

Not that any of her things was worth much. But many were as dear to her as priceless heirlooms. Photos of her grandparents, all dead now, her high school and community college diplomas, a childhood diary, a framed copy of her first paycheck, and other mementos that proved she'd more than survived her upbringing.

Without them, she felt rudderless and lost.

Failing to find even a remnant of Froggy hurt most of all. A gift from Mrs. Steen, a nurturing teacher who cared for and believed in Deanna, the frog symbolized a bright moment in an otherwise dismal year.

Deep sorrow for all she'd lost mingled with fresh anger—at herself, for getting involved with Rusty, and at him for the lies.

Tense and unhappy, she hugged herself. Mrs. Steen had taught her to count her blessings. Staring at the dark ceiling, Deanna reviewed them.

First, Bea and Vi, two loyal and supportive friends. Also lots of work friends. A car and two good jobs at the hotel. She owned property and would be reimbursed for the bungalow despite its old wiring. Dared to dream dreams no one could ever take from her: to make Oliver's Bed & Breakfast a reality, and someday, if she ever got her head on straight, to find a man she could love and trust.

Compared to some people, that was a lot.

Finding solace in that, she finally slept.

3

───────────

As soon as the forty-eight hour stretch ended Wednesday morning Hank and several of his crewmates headed for Rosemary's Breakfast Nook. Conveniently located a few blocks from the station, it was the go-to choice for eating and winding down.

They weren't the only ones who favored the restaurant. Even at just after eight a.m. the place was packed. Rosemary had saved their regular table, where Owen's girlfriend, Hallie, and Gus's lady, Wanda, sipped coffee and chatted. Hank and Max called out greetings, but the ladies were too busy exchanging more affectionate hellos with their men to notice.

Jana, a waitress around Hank's age, sashayed over with a flirty smile and a steaming pot of coffee. "Good morning, guys," she crooned as she filled the mugs. "Same as usual?"

After collecting the orders, she hustled to another table.

"Got any cool cars lined up at the garage?" Max asked Gus, who was nuzzling Wanda like he wanted her for breakfast.

He broke away and grinned. "A honey of a 1974 Pontiac Firebird—or she will be, once I finish with her."

Wanda rubbed her hands together. "If I can get away from the salon, I'm going to help. How about you, Max? Are you working on anything?"

A primo custom-wood furniture artist, Max was much in demand. "For starters, sleep like the dead until I wake up. Once I feel human again I'll finish an oak and teak side table for a customer."

Thanks to three calls the night before, none of them had gotten much shuteye.

Owen planned to take a nap, then divvy up the rest of his week between helping his sister and niece move into their own apartment and designing a new computer program.

When off-duty, Hank ran an appliance repair business that made house calls and accepted only jobs he could complete in a single visit. He made great money and the work varied enough to keep him on his toes. "No rest for me until tonight," he said. "I have two appointments today—a hot-water tank install and a garbage disposal replacement at Chrissy Henry's."

"Her again?" Gus hooted. "She sure keeps you busy. I'll bet my breakfast she's interested in more than your repair skills."

Hank agreed. Divorced and about forty, Chrissy was some ten years older than him. "She's not half-bad and I am tempted," he admitted. "Or I would be if she wasn't on the lookout for a new husband."

Max and Nate, unattached and content that way, each made a sign of the cross with their index fingers, the kind meant to ward off evil vampires.

Hank snorted, but he was with them. He wasn't exactly marriage material. A string of brief relationships proved it, the breakup with Gretchen the most recent.

After dating for some three months, a record for him, she'd brought up the subject of kids and asked if he wanted any. "Sure," he'd said. "Someday."

Gretchen figured he meant with her. He didn't, and should have clarified that he wasn't anywhere close to making that kind of commitment. He'd lost interest in her about the time she'd started dropping hints about the kind of ring she wanted. Not a pretty ending to their relationship, and he still felt lousy for hurting her. Disappointment should be his middle name.

"I don't have any other appointments booked yet, but that's how the business rolls," he added. "People will call if they need me. They always do."

"Did you and your brother figure out where to go on your vacay?" Max asked.

"Yep—camping and hiking in Southern Oregon and Northern California."

"He's driving down here?"

"That's right. We're taking the Scamp." The sweet sixteen-foot camper Hank had bought a year ago. "We leave two weeks from today." After burning the candle at both ends for months he was beyond ready.

Jana arrived with a tray loaded with food and all conversation ground to a halt.

Besides needing some serious R&R, Hank looked forward to hanging with his brother for a whole week. Hudson was five years older but they'd always been close. Which was why they got together a couple times a year despite living almost three hundred miles apart.

"Sounds like a great trip," Max said around a mouthful of his eggs. "With our early cold snap, the trees should be real pretty. I'm jealous, man."

For the dozenth time since they'd sat down the front door opened. To Hank's surprise Deanna Oliver and the elderly woman who'd offered her a place to bunk entered the restaurant.

He hadn't expected to see her, but now was as good a time as any to find out if she'd changed her mind about the benefit fund. If not, he'd work on getting her to apply.

With her hair neatly pulled back at the nape and the hint of a smile curling her full lips, she looked fresh and rested, not at all like a woman who'd lost her home two days ago. She sure was pretty.

"Isn't that Deanna Oliver?" Max asked.

"Yeah." Breakfast forgotten, Hank pushed his chair back and started toward her.

~

As Deanna and Bea hung up their jackets on the coat tree inside the front door, the older woman bracketed her mouth with her hand. "Here comes that handsome firefighter from the other day."

Deanna had noticed all on her own. Tall and lean with short, dark hair, big brown eyes, and a strong, square chin... What woman could possibly be immune to that?

But his broad shoulders and handsome face didn't mean he was a good man. She knew this, oh so well.

And yet she never seemed to learn.

Bea elbowed her. "Give him a big smile, Deanna."

Several diners caught the remark and eyed her curiously.

Embarrassed, she glanced away. Bea wanted her to fall in love and find the happily-ever-after she herself had lost. Between Deana's rotten judgment in men and the hole inside her caused by the devastating fire, she wasn't interested.

Hank reached her and nodded with the same somber expression he'd worn at the fire. "Hey."

She didn't smile, either. Ignoring the sigh of her wayward heart, she greeted him. "That's right—we're near the station. Is this your regular hangout?"

"My crewmates and I usually have breakfast here at the end of our double shift."

"You pulled a double shift?"

"Every week." He extended his hand to Bea. "I'm Hank."

To Deanna's surprise her friend blushed and gave him a flirtatious smile. "Petaluma Beasley, but call me Bea. Everyone does."

Hank gestured at the booth behind him. "Come on over and meet some of the crew who helped at the fire."

At the table he made the introductions. In person every man outshone his calendar photo, which was saying a lot. Hank was the most attractive of the bunch.

If that wasn't thrill enough, Deanna also met Gus's and Owen's girlfriends. She envied both women.

Bea continued to vamp, angling her head a saucy fraction. "If I'd known you were going to be here, I'd have brought my calendar for autographs."

"We'll catch you next time," Hank said, and the woman almost swooned.

Deanna barely smothered her laughter. Hank met her gaze and shook his head in shared amusement. She caught a whiff of his aftershave, something clean and fresh that reminded her of pine trees.

Because she wanted to lean in close and inhale the scent, she addressed firefighters at the table. "I owe you all a huge thanks for fighting to save my house and for keeping the bed and breakfast relatively intact."

"Credit Hank for protecting the bed & breakfast," Max said. "He may be our newest firefighter but he sure is good."

"Shut it," Hank muttered, bowing his head as if the praise made him uncomfortable.

"What brings you two here this morning?" Wanda asked.

Bea smiled. "Deanna's treating me to breakfast."

"After your hospitality the last two nights it's the least I can do."

The older woman scoffed and pointed her thumb at Deanna. "This one doesn't like to be beholden to anyone—not even her neighbor and friend. It's been my pleasure, Deanna."

While Bea chatted with Hank's crewmates he turned to Deanna. "Did you find Froggy?" he asked in a voice for her ears only.

He remembered, which touched her. But wishing she'd recovered the ceramic treasure and the rest of her possessions wouldn't change the fact that every-thing was gone.

Her sorrow bone-deep, she shook her head.

Hank squeezed her shoulder in a gesture of com-passion that for some reason helped, just as it had after the fire.

"Sorry to hear that. How are you doing otherwise?"

"I'm coping." Still feeling like an idiot for blindly accepting Rusty's assurances that he'd fixed the wiring, she decided not to mention that. "The bun-galow wasn't much, but it was mine, and..." Refusing to let her feelings get the best of her, she bumped past the pain. "The reimbursement from the insurance company will certainly help."

"Don't forget our benefit fund."

Again with that. "I don't need help, and I don't take charity."

He looked startled. "FYI, our fund isn't remotely like charity."

"It feels that way to me."

Muttering something about her being stubborn, he spread his hands in a "what can you do?" gesture. "Suit yourself. Are you staying at Bea's again tonight?"

Deanna shook her head. "I'll be at my friend Vi's for a few days. By then I'll have found a new place to live—cross your fingers. I have appointments to see a couple of places after breakfast today."

"What are you looking for?"

He seemed to genuinely care. Handsome and nice —a dangerous combination sure to shoot holes in her defenses if she weren't careful.

"Something close to the resort if possible," she said. "I don't need anything big or fancy." A server bustled past. Deanna glanced at the wall clock. "It's getting late. Bea and I need to eat."

Hank nodded. "Take care."

"I always do."

As Deanna and Bea moved toward an empty table she sensed he was checking her out. Something all guys were hardwired to do. Still, a thrill rippled through her.

Frowning, she sat down with her back to him. All the same she was acutely aware of his presence.

4

Deanna started her workday staffing the front desk at the Guff's Lake Resort Hotel. Taking care of guests and dealing with whatever else came up had taught her invaluable customer service skills unique to the hospitality industry, experience sure to come in handy when she opened Oliver's.

Later in the day she switched into server mode at the Hearthstone. Restaurant work was equally informative and with tips, paid much better.

Having worked steadily from the age of fourteen, she couldn't imagine lazing about—even on her days off. Both jobs made her feel productive and she enjoyed them.

Not so much today.

Eric, the front-desk manager old enough to be her father, greeted her with a sympathetic smile. Like everyone else working at the resort he'd heard about the fire. "How're you holding up, kiddo?"

"I've had better days, but don't worry, I can fake it with the best of them." She forced a bright smile. "See? Although today I may not need to." The lobby was deserted. "It sure is quiet in here."

"So far. Where are you going to live, Dee?"

"I wish I knew. I had two appointments this morning. One place was a total dump—moldy, drafty, and smelly. The other got snapped up before I even had a chance to see it."

"With the hot rental market here I'm not surprised."

"I am. Things are a lot different than the last time I rented an apartment." Some three years ago.

"Finding a place could take awhile."

Not what Deanna wanted to hear. Who had time to waste precious hours on that? "If you hear of anything in the area..."

"I'll let you know, but don't hold your breath. My wife and I re-upped the lease on our place and agreed to a bump in the rent we can hardly afford so we wouldn't have to go through what you are."

Glum, she leaned on the counter and rested her chin on her fist. "Maybe I should expand my search to other parts of town."

"I would."

On that dismal note, three phone lines lit up.

"Here we go," Eric said.

Pushing her worries aside Deanna shifted into front-desk mode. In no time she was too busy to think about anything but the here and now.

THANKS to unforeseen problems installing the hot-water tank, Hank didn't arrive at Chrissy Henry's until mid-afternoon. She liked to keep him company as he worked, which involved lots of chitchat, mostly on her part. As beat as he was, that suited him fine.

"I heard about the horrible fire at that poor

woman's home," she said while he was under the kitchen sink.

She would bring that up. Hank grimaced but wasn't really surprised. In Guff's Lake, news always traveled at warp speed.

From what he knew of Deanna, she'd bristle at being labeled "that poor woman." "It suc— We all feel bad," he replied. Him most of all. "But she seems resilient." More like hardheaded and too proud for her own good, but he wasn't going to say that. "I think she'll be all right."

"That's good to hear. Thank God no one was hurt."

"Amen. What have you been up to?" he asked, changing the subject.

Chrissy talked about her office job, then a recent shopping trip with a friend, and lots of other stuff that didn't require more than a perfunctory reply here and there.

It was nearly dark when he finished installing her new disposal. After flipping the switch a couple times to ensure the thing worked, he nodded. "You're all set."

"Thanks, Hank. I don't know what I'd do without you." She handed him a check and flashed a too-warm smile. "How about a beer?"

"Can't."

She put on a pouty face. "That's too bad. Another appointment?"

Not about to lie, he shook his head. "You're the last today."

"Ah—you have a date."

Hank thought of Deanna. Because face it, he was interested. Tough beans. Having messed up her life big time, he could never get together with her. Anyway, she probably had a boyfriend.

Then why wasn't she staying with him?

Regardless, she had enough on her mind without him complicating matters.

"Dinner plans," he explained, leaving out the fact that he planned to pick up fast food at Burger Mania, then head home to eat and crash. Better for them both if Chrissy thought he was involved.

She sighed. "Whoever she is, she's a lucky woman. Have fun."

Tonight, all he wanted was a solid night's sleep. He summoned a smile. "You know it."

5

When Rick left Friday morning for work at the office supplies store he managed, Vi turned to Deanna. "If you want to stay with us for a few more days..."

Deanna doubted her aching back could survive a third night on the sagging futon in the minuscule living room. Also, she didn't want to wear out her welcome. She shook her head. "You're sweet to offer but I made other plans."

Vi didn't argue. "I don't have to leave for work for over an hour," she said as she twisted her hair into a French braid.

She worked for the Guff's Lake Visitors and Convention Bureau. "We have eggs and bacon in the fridge. Let's have breakfast like when we roomed together—just the two of us. Unless you're looking at rentals again this morning."

"I am, but I have time for a quick cup of coffee."

They headed to the kitchen, where Deanna poured the coffee and her friend thoughtfully made her a bagel with cream cheese for the road.

"I sure hope you have better luck than yesterday," Vi said.

After losing out to renters who offered to pay more than the asking rent on two different apartments, Deanna had her doubts. "Let's hope. These rentals are on the east side of town where the competition is less fierce."

"That's a long way from the resort, but a girl's gotta do what she must. I'll cross my fingers that today is the day you find a new home. How many are you seeing?"

"Four—three apartments and a five-bedroom house with an available bedroom."

Val looked thoughtful. "Rooming with people you've never met could be interesting. Heck, you might meet a cute guy."

"Cute is for teenage boys," Deanna said.

"I disagree—Rick is pretty cute and he's all man." Vi's sigh was pure love.

"Good point." Although compared to Hank...

"I know that look, Dee. You've met someone. It's about time, but geez. I'm your best friend and you haven't said a word." Vi looked hurt.

"I did meet a guy," Deanna admitted. "But I don't think he's interested. And the truth is, I can't afford to be."

"You lost your home—the worst thing ever. But that doesn't mean you can't date."

"I don't want to."

"Because you think your judgment in men is seriously flawed." Vi's dismissive wave conveyed her opinion of that. "I'd like to wring the heck out of Rusty's thick neck and anyone else's who made you doubt yourself. And now, with his lies about the wiring... But don't get me started. Tell me about this mystery man you met."

"All right, but this stays between us, and you have to promise not to laugh."

"I won't say a word or laugh. Unless you've fallen for a big-time TV wrestler." Vi's lips twitched.

Deanna glanced at the firefighter calendar hanging on the wall.

"Too bad you lost your copy in the fire," Vi said. "Contact the fire department and ask if they have an extra you could buy. Come to think of it, I read that they sold out in record time. You'll have to wait until next year. In the meantime, when you need a hunky-guy fix feel free to drool over mine. We'll drool together. Don't tell Rick."

"He probably knows you spend all your time when he's not around staring at that calendar."

"Ha-ha. You were going to tell me about your new love interest."

"Don't use the 'L' word with me. I'm not going there again for a long, long time." Deanna flipped the pages backward to May.

"Ooh, Hank Gardener. Those melting eyes, that sexy smile... Looking at him every day for a whole month was a real treat."

"All that and he saved Oliver's."

"He's the one you're interested in? Get out! I love a man in uniform...or bare-chested. Especially when he's as buff as Hank."

Deanna agreed wholeheartedly. Tossing and turning on the uncomfortable futon last night, her mind hovering between wakefulness and sleep, she'd indulged in a wild fantasy featuring the two of them naked and tangled together.

A certain female part started to ache. Going without sex for a year had been difficult. "The day we met I was in shock from the fire and what had happened to the bungalow. But the second time..."

"You've seen him again?"

Deanna nodded. "When I took Bea to Rosemary's for breakfast the other morning. He and some of his crewmates were there."

"And?"

"He was friendly and seemed concerned about me. End of story."

Or would be if she could stop thinking about him. She glanced at her watch. "I need to scoot or I'll be late for my first appointment." She grabbed her purse and the suitcase she'd bought at Second Hand Rose, the second-hand store in town.

"If you find a place, let me know," Vi said at the door.

"I will. Thanks for letting me stay here—and for the bagel." Deanna hugged her, then left.

As it turned out, competition on the east side of town was equally as intense as near the lake. An hour, three apartments and one house later Deanna was still homeless.

And panicky. Where was she going to live?

With a good ninety minutes before she needed to clock in at work, she decided to stop for coffee at the Coffee Shack, which wasn't far from the resort, to think what to do. On the way she called Vi.

"It's me," she said. "Are you busy?"

"Not at all. You don't sound so good. No luck, huh?"

"I wish."

"What about the bedroom in the house?" Vi asked.

"Five college students live there, none of them over twenty. I'm not that much older but they seem so young."

"Eight years is a big difference."

"Still, I was ready to take the room. While we were discussing details a girl stopped by with a cashier's check for the rent and damage deposit."

"They'd already rented the room and didn't tell you?"

"They weren't sure she'd follow through."

Vi made a sound of disgust. "That's so unfair. Are you sure you don't want to stay with Rick and me tonight?"

"You need your privacy and I need mine. I'll book a room at the hotel." Two nights, max, was all Deanna could afford. She didn't get paid for another week, and not counting the money she'd set aside for an apartment rental, her bank balance had shrunk too low for comfort.

She couldn't even fall back on a credit card because she didn't have one. Having grown up with parents who were habitually in debt and broke, she'd always paid cash and had built up a safety net to prevent falling into a similar situation.

Now she needed to build it back up. Which meant frivolous spending was out.

It was either find a place soon or borrow an air mattress and sleeping bag from Vi and move into Oliver's. Which had two broken windows covered in plywood and no insulation. Not a stick of furniture, either, or a working kitchen. Add in this year's unusually cold fall, and nights in the drafty building were bound to be uncomfortably cold.

And no improvements in sight for the foreseeable future. For now Deanna's dream of restoring the bed & breakfast seemed far away.

"You never know, you could find something tomorrow," Vi said.

Deanna prayed her friend was right. She needed a better option than Oliver's, and fast.

~

READY FOR A COFFEE, Deanna parked in the Coffee Shack lot. As she unbuckled her seatbelt her phone rang. Matt, her insurance agent, was calling. He'd said Friday and here he was.

Eager to find out how much money she could expect, and by when—at last, some good news—she stayed in the car and picked up. "Hi, Matt. What can you tell me?"

"Before I answer that, I need additional information about the home you're planning to build to replace the one you lost," he said.

"I'm not going to rebuild—I'm going to use the money on the bed & breakfast next door."

"Oh? You didn't mention that before."

"I never realized it mattered."

"It does. When you rebuild we pay the replacement cost of all materials—the framing, fixtures, plumbing, and so on. But if you're going to use the funds elsewhere instead, we base your reimbursement on the cost of the original materials."

Deanna rubbed the space between her eyes. "I'm not sure I understand."

"Let me look through your information." She heard the rapid clatter of Matt's keyboard. "Your house was built in 1966 with no major improvements since. Is that correct?"

"The roof was fifteen years old, I think. My ex-boyfriend painted, weather-stripped the doors, and put new caulking around the windows. That's it."

"Then unfortunately, we can only reimburse you for what the building materials cost at the time they were purchased. Fifteen years ago for the roof and 1966 for the rest. Let's say the person who built the house paid five hundred dollars total for the windows. That's what we'll pay you."

In other words, Deanna wasn't going to get nearly as much money as she'd anticipated. She slumped in her seat. "I see."

"At least you'll get something for the bungalow, and after you meet the deductible, you're covered for any materials used to repair the damage to the bed & breakfast. I'll need to do some research. As soon as I calculate the amount I'll get back to you."

Shaken and upset by this latest bump in the road, Deanna disconnected. Forget coffee—she needed Bea. She called to let her friend know she was coming, then drove straight there.

Refusing to even glance toward her own property —like a gaping wound, the sight hurt almost too much to bear—she parked in front of Bea's. Before she exited the car, the woman opened her door in welcome.

"Sit down and tell me what's happened," she said when Deanna entered the house.

By the time Deanna had explained the situation she'd thought of a solution to her money woes. "My lot is pretty big, and Guff's Lake is growing," she said. "What if I sell the property where the bungalow stood?"

"I was going to suggest the same thing," Bea said. "You've always been practical—it's one of the things I admire most about you."

Except when it came to men.

"I happen to know something about subdividing property," Bea went on. "Richard was in the housing development business, you know."

"I remember. Tell me what I need to do."

"First, get a survey of the property. Once you determine the size of the lot you want to sell—it should be big enough to build on—you'll need to find a buyer. That means hiring a real estate agent, or you could advertise and sell on your own. All of which could take time."

Deanna had precious little of that. The very process of finding and hiring an expert to subdivide the lot would require energy and effort—and more money. Not knowing anything about advertising and selling land meant she also had to hire someone for that, too.

Just thinking about the added burden ahead gave her a headache on top of her heartache.

"Thanks for the info, Bea. I should go or I'll be late for work."

Bea gave her a big hug. "Take heart, Deanna. You're right—the population here expands every year. This is a prime location to build on, and your land could sell fast. I'm almost sure it will."

It was an unwritten rule that poker was not played at the station. No one including Captain Comings knew where or why the ban had originated. To compensate, the crew had set up a standing Friday night game that rotated from house to house. Anyone from the station was welcome. Sometimes ten people showed, sometimes two or three.

Hank had hosted tonight's game. The fun had ended around ten. Whistling, Hank filled a bag with cigar butts and beer bottles into the trash and returned the card tables and chairs to the storage closet.

He was sprawled on the sofa munching leftover chips, sipping a beer, and channel-surfing when his cell rang with a call from Hudson. Grinning, Hank muted the volume on the tube and answered. "Yo."

"Hey, little brother. What's shakin'?"

"Nothing much—just chillin' after the poker game. Six guys showed."

"A respectable number. How'd you do?"

"Not well enough to win the fourteen-dollar pot. That went to Max."

"Again? Better luck next time. Hate to be the

bearer of bad news at this late date, but I have to cancel our hiking trip."

Hudson had never done this before. Hank sat up straight. "Anything wrong?"

"My partner broke his leg this morning and I can't leave the clinic without a veterinarian."

Hank swore. "How'd that happen?"

"One of our cat patient's owners moved a basket of magazines out of the way to make room for her kitty carrier. Blake was reading a chart instead of watching where he was going. He tripped over the basket."

"Must've been some fall. I'll bet that caused pandemonium."

"Like you wouldn't believe. It would've been funny if his femur hadn't snapped."

All firefighters at GLFD were certified paramedics and rotated between firefighting and medical duties. Between that and Hank's previous job as a full-time paramedic he'd seen his share of broken bones. "Nasty," he said. "The leg is in traction, right?"

"For at least the next forty-eight to seventy-two hours. Beyond that we don't know, except that he probably won't be putting any weight on it for a while."

"Figured as much. I won't lie, I'm disappointed."

"You and me both. I put the word out for a locum tenens—a vet to fill in while I'm away—but on such short notice I haven't found anyone. I know you set your vacation a year in advance and can't reschedule, but if there's any chance..."

"There isn't."

Hank heard feminine laughter in the background. "Where are you, man?"

"At my place. I was supposed to cook dinner for Mel tonight, but with Blake out I ended up working until after eight. She let herself in and cooked for me instead."

"Nice going. She has a key to your place, huh?"

"Yep, and I have hers."

Sounded as if things were getting serious. "You two have been going out for what—six months? That's an all-time record for a Gardener man. Twice mine."

Hank's brother let out a low laugh. "What can I say? I really like her. Also she's pretty and smells good."

"Give me the phone and stop that." Melanie squealed the last two words, and Hank pictured her batting Hudson away. "Hi, Hank," she said.

"Hey, Mel." They'd talked a couple times, but had never met face to face. If things continued as they were, that would change. "Is my brother treating you all right?"

"No complaints so far."

"Make sure to keep him in line."

"I will. 'Bye."

Hudson came back on the phone. "Gotta run. We'll get together at Christmas—I'll drive down. Count on it."

No longer interested watching in the tube, Hank shut it off. His plans had been canceled but not his vacation. He considered doing the trip solo, then nixed the idea. He already spent enough time in his own company.

Yet he needed a real break from both firefighting and his appliance repair business, something different from the usual that was both challenging and appealing. But what?

At the moment Hank had no idea. He wasn't worried—he had the weekend and a couple days next week to figure it out. Something interesting was bound to come up.

SATURDAY NIGHT HANK scrapped his plans to meet Max and Ethan at Lucky Joe's for an evening of meeting women and dancing. If that wasn't crazy enough, he traded his standard jeans and T-shirt for dress pants, a dress shirt, and leather shoes. Standard attire for dinner at the classy Hearthstone Restaurant.

All to find out how Deanna was doing. She'd been in his thoughts a lot. He wanted to make things easier for her, but at Rosemary's the other day the mere mention of the benefit fund had offended her.

She'd rejected the suggestion outright when she could obviously use the cash. Hell, anyone in her situation would.

Hank needed her to change her mind, apply for help, and accept the money. Not just for her sake, but to salve his guilt-ridden conscience. Otherwise he'd never find peace of mind.

At seven-thirty the place was packed, mostly with locals. He recognized several faces, even knew a few names. As the attractive, young hostess led him to a table, he nodded hellos.

Busy servers wielded trays laden with great-smelling food. Flickering candles and linen-clad tables, and plush carpet and soundproofing muffled the conversation, providing an atmosphere of privacy and intimacy. People from miles around came here for romantic dinners and special occasions.

The hostess smiled warmly and set a menu in front of him. As eager as he was to look it over and choose something to fill his empty belly, the sight of

Deanna distracted him. At a table nearby with her back to him, she was delivering cocktails and appetizers to a table of half a dozen men in suits and ties.

Her hair was neatly tied back as it had been the other day at Rosemary's. The fitted white blouse of her server uniform emphasized her slender waist, and loose, dark trousers clung to her gently rounded hips and hinted at long legs. It wasn't exactly a sexy outfit but she looked hot.

Hank didn't care for the male interest she generated, visible even from a distance.

A man wearing a small gold nametag identifying him as "Caleb" filled his glass with water and set a basket of warm bread on the table. "Is there a problem, sir? Your server, Deanna, will be with you shortly. Can I bring you something to eat or drink in the meantime?"

Realizing he was scowling, Hank offered a friendly expression. "I'll wait for her."

Caleb stopped beside her and nodded his chin Hank's way.

Eyes widening in surprise, Deanna signaled she'd be right over. She moved toward him at the rapid clip she seemed to prefer.

"Hi," she said, smiling.

The other day he hadn't noticed the color of her eyes. Blue-gray, framed by thick, sooty lashes—beautiful. He lost himself in them until she flushed and glanced away.

"Are you meeting someone for dinner?" she asked.

He shook his head. "I haven't eaten here in a while and I figured it was time to find out if the food is as good as I remember. Also, I wanted to see you."

"Me." She frowned. "What for? How did you know I was here?"

He skirted the first question and answered the second. "You mentioned that you worked at the hotel the day of the fire. I called the main number and asked where to find you."

"Do you need something from me?"

Yeah, and it had nothing to do with convincing her to use the benefit fund. He wanted to know if she tasted as good as she looked.

Bad idea. She'd suffered enough on his account.

"I've been thinking about you, wondering if you found a place to live," he said. That was the truth.

"No, and I'm getting desperate. This morning I even called back a dumpy place I looked at and rejected last week. It was already rented." Anxiety flared in her eyes. "Please tell me you know of an available apartment."

Hank shook his head. "I asked around but no one knows of a place. "

"Oh, well." A weary sigh slipped out. "I also got depressing news from my insurance agent."

If she wasn't getting the funds she needed, maybe she'd reconsider the benefit fund. But this seemed the wrong time to bring that up. "What happened?" he asked.

"It's complicated and I don't have time to explain. We're really busy tonight and I need to see to other guests, but first let me tell you about tonight's specials."

She rattled through a list of impressive-sounding dishes that had him salivating.

On hearing his selection she flashed a smile. "I figured you for a steak man. You made a great choice."

She headed for another table. Moments later Caleb delivered the wine and Hank tucked into the bread.

"Still staying with that friend of yours?" he asked when she delivered his calamari and dip appetizer.

"You mean Vi?" She shook her head. "She and her boyfriend just moved in together and their place is hardly big enough for the two of them."

He nodded. "If I was your boyfriend, I'd want you to bunk with me."

"Rusty and I aren't together anymore."

Single, then. Hank exhaled the breath he'd been holding.

Deanna's flattened lips warned him away from prying questions. He asked anyway. "Bad breakup?"

"Bad from the start. He said he was divorced. He wasn't."

"Ouch."

One shoulder lifted and fell. "It's been a year. I'm over him now."

Maybe, but it was obvious she still hurt. "I've been single about as long as you."

"Did your ex lie to you, too?"

He wasn't about to get into the thing with Gretchen. "It just didn't work out," he summarized.

A man at a nearby table signaled for the check and Deanna headed off again. She was non-stop busy, too intent on her job to notice him staring. She had a friendly way about her that her customers responded well to. Hank admired that. He tended to be more reserved, which often made others ill at ease.

Shortly after Caleb removed Hank's empty appetizer plate, Deanna delivered the steak and the side dishes.

Hank's mouth watered. "This looks and smells delicious."

Laughter transformed her from pretty to knockout.

"What's so funny?" he asked, half-grinning himself.

"Your enthusiasm for the food. When you rub your stomach and lick your lips, I picture you as a little boy, doing the same things."

One of his warmest memories stemmed from the time his mother had been in town on his birthday and had baked him a cake. She didn't cook often and had been tickled when the cake had turned out and he'd licked his lips and asked for seconds. "I sure did."

"I knew it." Her smile widened. "How about another glass of wine?"

He shook his head. "I'm good."

"You're going to love this steak," she added. "The meat is so tender it melts in your mouth."

Since he was a guy, his mind went straight to ways she could melt him with her mouth. His cock jumped to attention. Giving himself a mental eye roll he leaned his forearms on the table. "What time do you get off?"

"We close at nine—about fifteen minutes from now—but you're already here, so feel free to linger as long as you like."

"Do you have to stick around until every customer is gone?"

She shook her head. "Only until the people in my station leave, which could be anytime between now and nine forty-five."

"I'll bet you'll be glad to sit down."

"Definitely. Not counting breaks I've been on my feet since eleven this morning."

"That's quite a shift."

"Yours is worse."

"True that. Today was no picnic, either. I didn't realize the dining room was open for lunch this time of year."

"It isn't. I start here at five. From eleven to four I'm at the front desk."

"That makes for a long day."

"I'm used to it. I've been balancing the two positions for the last ten years—since I was eighteen. You should eat while the food is hot. I need to check on my other customers."

By the time he finished his meal the dining room crowd had thinned considerably. He signaled Deanna over. "That was a great dinner."

"Told you. Do you have room for dessert?"

The dessert he wanted had nothing to do with food and everything to do with Deanna. Hank was not going there. He shook his head.

His plan to talk more about the benefit fund had failed. She'd been too busy. He'd pay and leave and try again another time. His mouth had other ideas. "Can I buy you a drink after work?"

Her eyebrows jumped. "If you're asking me out, you shouldn't. I'm not in a good place right now."

No kidding. She'd just lost her house. But over drinks he'd have her undivided attention and just might persuade her to apply for the money she needed. Yeah, that could work.

"Trust me, you wouldn't want to go out with me anyway," he said. "I'm here and the lounge is across the lobby, and I'm curious about the insurance problem you mentioned. I figured you might want to unwind. No big deal."

Only it was, even more than convincing her to use the benefit fund. Go figure.

Her open face was easy to read and he could almost see her mind whirring while she considered the offer.

Finally she nodded. "All right, I'll meet you there when I finish up here. But I'll pay for my own drink."

Usually when Deanna clocked out and left the Hearthstone she wanted nothing more than to kick off her shoes, put her feet up, and turn on TV.

Not tonight. Friendly, handsome guys had always been her weakness—even when she knew better— and meeting Hank for a drink excited her.

It's not a date, she reminded herself, because she wasn't sure she wanted that. Despite what she'd told him, she wasn't totally shutting the door on their seeing each other. First she needed to know him better, which was why she was here.

As always on a Saturday night, the lounge was crowded. Finding him might take a moment. It didn't. As if guided by some magnetic force, she located him right away. He'd snagged a booth on the far side of the room.

As she made her way toward him several women following her gaze gave her envious looks. But then, Hank was the best-looking man in the room. And those shoulders—strong and so broad that they strained his dress shirt when he moved.

Her stomach flip-flopped as it hadn't in too long to

remember. That worried her. She shouldn't do this, ought to plead exhaustion and tell him she'd changed her mind.

He smiled so widely that the outer corners of his eyes crinkled, as if the sight of her pleased him immensely.

Like a sun-starved flower she basked in his warmth and forgot all about backing out.

A frosty beer mug sat in front of him. As soon as Deanna slid into the booth across from him he signaled Amelia, a forty-something cocktail waitress Deanna had known for years.

Amelia greeted Deanna with a ready smile and a speculative look. "Hey, Dee."

Deanna could just imagine what the woman was thinking. Striving to slake her curiosity, she returned the smile. "This isn't a date. Meet Hank Gardener, one of the firefighters who saved Oliver's."

Amelia studied Hank. "I recognize you from the firefighter calendar, but I didn't know the rest. You're a hero, for sure. What can I get you, Dee?"

"A glass of white wine and nachos with the works."

"You bet." Amelia headed off.

"Hungry, are you?" Hank's eyes twinkled.

"I haven't eaten since my four o'clock break. And in case you didn't notice, tonight I ran my fanny off."

"I noticed."

His dark gaze flitted over her. Her nipples tingled. Geesh. "At dinner you mentioned something about today being no picnic for you, either," she said. "I thought you worked Mondays and Tuesdays."

"At the station. I also own a side business. Small household repairs."

"Two jobs—wow." Most of the men with whom Deanna had been involved had worked one, if that.

"During those five days off I need something to fill the time. Most of my crewmates do the same thing. And hey, you also work two jobs."

"Yes, but they're both connected to the hospitality industry. Where is your shop located?"

"It's a house-call-only business so I don't need a shop. I only accept work I can finish in one day or less. Bigger jobs get referred out."

"You go to the customer—there's a terrific idea."

"People seem to like it. Today I had four calls and they took up the whole day. I didn't even have time for my ten-mile run."

"Ten miles?"

"Except when I go with the guys. Then it's more like five miles. Daily distance running has always been my thing."

Talk about impressive. "I can't even imagine," Deanna said. "I could maybe run halfway around a track—if someone bribed me with a gooey dessert."

Hank chuckled and gave a modest shrug. "I did cross-country in high school and college."

Fighting fires, fixing appliances, distance running —was there nothing the man couldn't do?

"Tell me about the insurance complications you mentioned earlier," he said.

"It has to do with my decision not to rebuild the bungalow. According to my insurance agent, that changes everything. My policy will only cover the original cost of the materials, and I won't get nearly as much money as I thought. I'm going to subdivide and sell part of the property. I'll use what I make to fix up Oliver's."

"Smart."

Her order arrived. One look at the mountain of nachos and she slid the platter toward the middle of the table. "This is way too much for one person. Help yourself."

"You saw the huge meal I polished off earlier. Maybe later."

Deanna dug in. "This is yummy," she said around a mouthful.

Hank grinned. "I can see that. If you're not sleeping at your friend's tonight, where are you staying?"

Not what she wanted to think about right now. She forced a cheerful tone. "Right here. All I have to do is walk over to my room on the opposite side of the hotel."

"That's convenient."

"Sure is."

Hank fiddled with his mug and she knew he still felt bad about the loss of her home.

She touched his rock-hard forearm. "Don't worry about me. I'll survive."

His big, warm hand covered hers, and something dangerous and electric passed between them. There went her nipples again. Her entire body joined in, thrumming and expectant for male attention at last. Unnerved, she pulled free.

Hank cleared his throat. " You're tough, all right and strong is good, but your life would be easier with assistance from the benefit fund."

Not wanting anything to do with that money, Deanna compressed her lips. "What part of 'No, thanks' don't you understand?"

"And people call me hard-headed."

"Without my so-called hard head, I wouldn't be where I am now."

"Whatever. Just promise me one thing—if you need help, swallow your pride and ask for it."

She needed him to understand. "This is about way

more than pride. I grew up with parents who asked for handouts on a regular basis. It was embarrassing, and I made a promise to myself to make my own way no matter what. So please, stop asking."

"Got it—from now on, the benefit fund is off-limits."

By way of thanks, she tipped her wine glass his way.

Hank sipped his beer. She couldn't help but notice how his big hand dwarfed the mug. Maybe it was the wine—she never had learned to nurse a drink—but something about his thick fingers and clean, blunt nails turned her on.

But then, everything about Hank Gardener did. Already she liked him too much for her own good.

"A couple years ago I bought the house I'd rented since I joined GLFD," he said. "Like your B&B, it had good bones but needed work. I've spent a chunk of money and countless hours fixing it up."

"I can identify—and I envy you for having the job behind you."

"I haven't finished by a long shot, but for now it'll do."

"When I bought my property, the appraiser told me the wiring was old and should be replaced within the next year," Deanna said. "Knowing what I know now, it's a wonder I ever got a mortgage."

"I read the report."

Wishing she'd never trusted Rusty to fix the problem—there it was again, the "t" word—she shook her head. "I sure have made mistakes. If I could only go back and relive the last two years..."

"I hear that. Hindsight is always crystal clear. What would you have done differently?"

"Run the other way the first time Rusty asked me

out." Talking about him made Deanna feel naïve to the point of stupidity. "You probably don't want to hear about this."

"Actually, I do."

The way Hank looked at her made her feel special, as if she were the most important person in the room. For that reason she decided to tell the story, even if it if did expose her for the fool she'd been.

"We met at Rogue Valley Community College, where we were both enrolled in the business program," she began. "Rusty said he was divorced and looking to start his life over. We shared our dreams—mine to open Oliver's, his to start his own construction business." Those had been heady days of excitement. And love. Deanna had believed she'd finally met the perfect man, and Rusty seemed to feel the same about her.

"Around the time we graduated he started talking marriage. We looked for a place together. I never expected to find a bungalow and a vacant bed & breakfast on one plot of land. Both needed tons of work, but the price was right.

"I'd been saving up to buy my own house since I started here at the hotel, and I had a nice nest egg. Rusty worked part-time at a small construction company. Between his low earnings and bad credit he couldn't qualify for a mortgage, so we made a deal. I'd put up the money for the down payment and take out the mortgage in my name. He'd contribute his share through sweat equity and split the monthly payments with me."

Hank nodded. "Not a bad plan."

"That's what I thought." She bit her lip.

"He bailed on you."

"The first few months were okay. He kept his part-time job and spent the rest of his time working on the bungalow so that we could move in." Now for the most humiliating piece of the story. "He was supposed to replace the bungalow's wiring. When he said the job was done, there was no reason not to believe him. You know where that led. What a great guy, huh?"

The couple at the adjacent booth shot Deanna curious looks, and she realized her voice had risen. Small wonder—she was still fuming over Rusty's stunt. She sucked in and blew out a calming breath.

Hank looked incredulous. "Are you effing serious?"

"I'm afraid so."

"That kind of job requires skill, experience, and a license. Why would he lie?"

"I've asked myself that over and over. Maybe he wanted me to think he was a construction god, or he's a pathological liar. All I know is, I'm lucky he's out of my life."

She meant that. No telling what other havoc he'd have left in his wake if he'd stuck around. "Anyway, once we moved into the bungalow he started on the B&B. He got as far as pulling up the carpet and tearing out the walls before he slacked off."

"Now that, I understand," Hank said. "He burned himself out working two demanding jobs."

"Not quite. Long story short, instead of being divorced, it turned out he and his wife were separated. Without my knowing, he started seeing Lynn again." To wash away the bitter taste in her mouth, Deanna drained her glass.

Hank swore. "You kicked him to the curb, right?"

"That very night. I heard later that Lynn was pregnant. Rusty quit his job and gave up construction for good. Now he works for his wife's father at a tire store."

"Remind me not to patronize that place."

"None of this is her father's fault."

"No, but if I met Rusty I'd punch him one."

Hank's righteous indignation on Deanna's behalf felt good. "I wouldn't stop you," she said.

He eyed the nachos. "Sure you don't want those?"

"I've had enough. I thought you were too full."

"Not anymore. Credit my high metabolism. You must have it, too. You're thin."

"That's from stress. Some people eat. I lose my appetite."

A pained look crossed his face. "You have a lot on your plate, for sure."

"Two jobs, losing my house, finding a place to live, renovating the bed & breakfast—you said it. If you don't eat this, it'll go to waste."

"Can't let that happen. I could use some coffee to go with these. How about you?"

She shouldn't, but Hank was difficult to resist. With her screwy judgment, that probably meant she should walk the other way. But even if she didn't know him that well and even though rehashing the past had opened old wounds, Hank somehow made her troubles seem far away. Especially when he focused solely on her. He was such an amazing guy. She stayed right where she was.

One corner of his mouth hitched up as if he'd read her mind and approved, and she couldn't help but smile. "Coffee sounds good."

~

WHAT WAS HE DOING, chatting up Deanna when for her sake he should get out of here? Hank silently chided himself. His plan to convince her to use the benefit plan had failed and with it his chance to placate his conscience.

At the same time he enjoyed being with her, more than with any woman in a long while. She wasn't having a bad time, either. Her ex had put her through the wringer but talking about it had done her some good. She seemed more relaxed than when she'd sat down.

"What time do you work tomorrow?" he asked.

"Same as every day—eleven a.m. till around ninethirty p.m., Wednesday through Sunday. I have Mondays and Tuesdays off."

"That's a long workweek. When was the last time you had a vacation?"

"Not in a very long time." She laughed without much humor. "The truth is, I've never had a real vacation."

He couldn't believe that. "I'm no employment specialist, but I do know it's illegal not to give a full-time employee time off."

"Yes, and by law I'm required to take two weeks off per year, including a block of no less than five consecutive days. I still work, just not at the hotel."

"Doing what?"

"I used to temp to earn extra money."

"Surely the pay here isn't that bad."

"It's pretty good, especially with the tips I earn. But remember, I was saving for a down payment. Since buying the property I've spent most of my spare time working on Oliver's. Although now..." Her brow wrinkled and she exhaled a heavy breath. "Until I find a place to live, that's on hold."

He was sorry he'd brought up the subject.

"When was your last vacation?" she asked.

"This past Christmas. I was supposed to go hiking

and camping with Hudson—my brother—the week after next, only he canceled on me."

"What happened?"

"He's a veterinarian up in Portland at a two-man practice. His partner broke his leg. Hudson can't leave the clinic without another vet there."

"That's a shame. Is there someone else to go with?"

Hank shook his head. "Too late for that. I can't change the dates of my vacation and I haven't decided how to fill the time. All I know is, I'll be taking a break from both jobs."

"Sleeping in and lazing around with a good book sounds pretty good to me."

"One day of that and I'd go crazy."

She smiled. "After a day or two, so would I."

He almost lost himself in her eyes. "Has anyone ever told you what a great smile you have?"

"I've heard it a time or two, usually as a pick-up line."

"I mean it. Your whole face lights up."

The smile bloomed again. "Can I ask you something?"

"Shoot."

"This is purely out of curiosity and has to do with a comment you made at the restaurant. Why wouldn't I want to go out with you?"

For starters because his mistakes had cost her her home. But if he admitted that she'd look at him with hatred instead of warmth. She'd never let him help her, either. "I'm not the nicest guy around," he said. "Ask any woman I've been involved with."

"Don't tell me you cheated."

"I wouldn't do that."

"You borrowed money and didn't pay it back?"

"Borrow mon— Where are you coming up with this stuff?"

"Personal experience."

"You mean Rusty."

"And a couple guys before him."

Hank shook his head. "You know some real jerks."

"Sad but true. I seem to be a magnet for them. What's your issue?"

The biggie? Disappointing any woman who'd ever cared for him, but he wasn't getting into that. "I don't have much luck with lasting relationships."

She gave a knowing nod. "A love 'em, leave 'em man."

"Some might say that, although it's never my intention starting out."

"My inner trust-o-meter is way out of whack," she said. "I also have a bad habit of jumping into relationships right away. That's why I created my eight-date rule—no action until the eighth date. If I'd made that rule before I started dating with Rusty, he would have moved on to someone else and I'd be a lot better off now."

"Why the eighth date? Don't most people have a three-date rule?"

"That's too soon for me. I need to get to know a man without sex clouding my judgment. If he sticks with me that long then maybe we have something to build on." In a lower voice she added, "And maybe I won't get my heart broken."

Hank's protective hackles rose. "For what it's worth, I think Rusty's a damn fool."

He held Deanna's startled gaze, watched her eyes soften and warm. Her lips parted a fraction and he wanted to kiss her so bad.

Ducking her head, she smoothed her napkin on the table. "It's late. I should go."

Hank checked his watch. Nearly midnight. He was surprised how much time had passed. "Sit tight while I settle up with Amelia." He stood.

"Wait." Deanna opened her purse and pulled out a twenty.

He shook his head. "Put that away."

"We agreed that I'd pay for my own food and drink."

He wasn't about to let her do that. If he couldn't convince her to access the benefit fund he would help her in other ways. Starting tonight. "Next time. I'll be back."

8

———————

"You don't need to walk me to my room," Deanna said as she and Hank crossed the lobby toward the opposite side of the hotel.

"I'm a guy—it's what I do." His cockeyed grin coaxed out a smile of her own and she let him take her hand. "I enjoyed tonight," he said.

"Even when I talked about Rusty?"

"Not that, but the rest."

"Me, too. It was good to forget my situation for a few hours."

Hank dropped her hand and bowed his shoulders as if suddenly weighted down. "I'd like to do more to help. You don't want money—okay. What else can I do?"

"What I really need is a place to live... But you know that." With a sigh, she shared what she saw as her last resort. "If I don't find something in the next few days, I'll have to move into my bed & breakfast."

"In its current condition?"

"It has running water, working bathrooms, and electricity. With a camping stove and bedding I can make it work."

"Cooking indoors with a camping stove is dangerous. You don't want to end up with carbon monoxide poisoning."

Good point.

"What did the appraiser say about the B&B's wiring?"

"The same as he did about the bungalow—it's old and should be replaced in the near future." She sighed. "I probably shouldn't use it, huh?"

"A second inspection can't hurt. I do them all the time in both commercial and public buildings. It's part of my job as a firefighter. I can take a look tomorrow."

He'd already done enough. She didn't want to be beholden to him. "I'm sure you have better things to do," she said.

"Sunday is my day off. I don't have anything scheduled except a run."

"A day off is for relaxing. You don't owe me anything, Hank."

He frowned at the patterned carpet and muttered something that sounded like, "The hell I don't."

Before she could wonder about that he lightened his expression. "I like you, Deanna. Let me do this small thing."

She got all warm inside. Suspicion quickly followed and she hardened her heart and narrowed her eyes. "What would you want in return?"

He winced. "When you mentioned trust issues, you weren't kidding. What I want is for you to be safe."

Hank's guileless look convinced her. He really did like her and he wanted her to be safe, which were about the nicest things any man had ever said.

Her wayward heart started to melt. She hid her feelings under a frown of her own. "Okay. If you want to look in the morning I'll meet you there."

"You have another long day tomorrow—you need

rest. Give me the key. I'll let myself in and call you when I finish. Then you won't have to get up so early."

"I'm usually up by seven-thirty or eight," she said. "I could easily meet you at nine-thirty. But I can give you the key." She fished it from her purse.

Hank pocketed it and they turned down a softly lit hallway. "Sure is quiet on this side of the hotel," he said.

"Because at the moment these rooms are all vacant. When ski season hits in mid-November we'll be booked solid through next September." She stopped in front of the door to her room. "This is mine. Good night—and thanks for the nachos and wine. "

"Thanks for the company. You're an interesting woman and easy to talk to."

Interesting and easy to talk to? Another first from a man. So far Hank was batting a thousand. Glowing inside Deanna stood on her toes and kissed his cheek. He turned his head so that his mouth hovered less than an inch from hers. So close, she saw the fine bristles of new beard on his face. Felt his warm coffee breath on her cheek. And knew she'd die if he didn't kiss her.

On their own, her eyelids lowered. He cupped her face between his big hands, but nothing more happened.

After several frustrating seconds she tugged him down and made the contact she craved.

He groaned and wrapped his arms around her. Warm, strong, and solid, he smelled faintly of fresh air, pine, and man. Way too soon he pulled back to study her with his melted chocolate eyes, then kissed her again.

Deanna quickly caught fire. Equally greedy, and

hungry, Hank clasped her hips and anchored her against his erection.

Already aching for him, she considered inviting him into her room.

The strength of her need scared her. She broke away and pushed against his chest. "I need to go in now."

"Your eight-date rule—right." He released her.

"This wasn't a date," she reminded him—and herself.

"That was never my intention, either, I promise you. But despite ourselves, it sure felt like one."

"It wasn't. Good night." She stepped through the door, then closed and locked it.

~

AS IF LOSING Deanna 's home wasn't enough, Hank now lusted for her. "Nice going, ass-wipe," he muttered as he sped through the darkness toward home.

But damn, she was impossible to resist. Soft mouth, long legs, hungry looks... Responsive, too, matching him with equal heat. She'd shown him a glimpse of her passion.

A glimpse that wasn't nearly enough. He imagined loving her to the brink of orgasm, reveling in her frantic need, then burying himself in her moist heat...

His body hard and primed, he shifted in his seat. Cut off the fantasy and set his jaw. He had no business wanting her or fooling around with her—or getting involved. Period.

Under normal circumstances he'd disappear from her life and she'd soon forget him. But normal didn't apply to him and Deanna—not when for his own peace of mind he needed to atone for his sins by helping her out. Even if she didn't want that.

There must be a way to appease his conscience and also keep his distance. He needed to find it.

As he pulled up the driveway the motion detector house lights blinked on, flooding the blacktop, house, and yard with harsh, bright light. Hank parked the CRV beside the garage and trudged inside.

He was too keyed up to sleep. He needed to clear his head, to run. His favorite way—alone. The crisp, clear night made for near-perfect conditions. In no time he was sitting on the bench by the kitchen door, clipping illuminated spurs to the heels of his Asics. He fastened a glowing wrist link on each arm and secured a runner's headlight around his forehead. After slipping on sports earmuffs and a pair of lightweight thermal gloves, he was ready to roll.

He jogged up the street, then crossed to the vast, hilly meadow he knew as well as his own palm. Sure-footed, he upped his pace, eating up the dark ground until the brisk air stung his face, the lights of the houses in the area faded away, and he was truly alone. Somewhere nearby an owl hooted, and in the distance two dogs traded barks.

After a time his mind emptied and he simply ran until his leg muscles ached and the breath began to whoosh from his lungs in painful gasps. Looping around, he headed toward home.

He was almost there when the solution to his problems popped into his mind with no effort at all— just as they always had when he pushed himself to the brink of collapse.

He'd figured out a way to salve his conscience and offer Deanna help she couldn't refuse, both without subjecting himself to temptation.

Pleased with his plan he cooled down, guzzled water, ate again, and showered. His last thought before sleep claimed him was that he couldn't wait to see the surprised look on her face when he told her about it.

9

———

Waking up in her hotel room Sunday morning Deanna's first thoughts were of Hank and his bone-melting kisses. He sure knew how to rev a girl up.

But she needed to slow down—way down. Yes, she knew him better now, but not well enough to get physical. Last night had been a momentary lapse in judgment, one she wouldn't repeat anytime soon.

But such a nice lapse... "Stop it!" she ordered as she headed for the bathroom to shower and dress.

No matter how tender and warm she felt this morning, she was through leading with her heart. From now on her brain was in charge. If and when Hank proved to be as decent and straightforward as he seemed, if he was willing to wait, then... Her whole body thrilled at the idea of what could happen then.

In the middle of a dreamy sigh she cut herself off. "Eight dates, remember? We haven't even had one."

"Where are you headed?" Eric asked as she headed across the lobby after breakfasting at the hotel's coffee bar.

"I'm meeting Hank."

Her boss nodded. "The firefighter you hung out with in the lounge."

"You know about that?" Figured. News spread among the hotel employees as fast as it did through the town of Guff's Lake.

Eager to quell the rumor mill, she explained. "He happens to be inspecting the wiring at my B&B. Don't worry—I'll be back in time to clock in."

"See you then. Have fun."

The last thing Deanna needed was for people to think she and Hank were dating when they weren't. Not yet, anyway.

However, if he asked her out...

Big if.

"This is a safety thing, not a date."

Eric's teasing grin faded. "Okay."

A ringing phone at the front desk put an end to the conversation.

She exited the hotel. To ward off the chill of the damp, gray morning she zipped the winter parka she'd bought at Second Hand Rose.

He was waiting for her near the pile of debris. Still unable to bear looking at it, Deanna pinned her gaze on him. Dressed all in black—hoodie, jeans, and his bulging briefcase—he looked formidable and undeniably handsome, like the hero of a dystopian movie.

A comforting hug sure would be nice. Deanna longed to toss her resolve away and step into the shelter of Hank's strength and warmth. Forget her troubles and enjoy more of what they'd shared last night. But she was not going to give in.

She stopped some distance away. "Good morning," she said, polite but reserved.

Equally aloof, he gave a curt nod. "Hey." Clouded breath accompanied his greeting.

"This is only the first week of October—but it's so cold." Reminding herself to buy a hat and pair of gloves, she shoved her hands in her pockets.

"Thanks to the biting wind." Hank gestured at the jumble of burned timber and charred sink and bed springs. "Who's going to clean up this mess?"

"I asked my insurance agent to recommend someone, but I haven't heard back."

"If you want names and numbers, I know several guys in that line of work."

"Yes, please. Have you been waiting long?"

He shook his head. "Less than five minutes." He returned her key.

"And?" she said, crossing her fingers.

His grim expression alerted her to the bad news she'd expected. He opened the black briefcase and extracted the inspection report. "In a nutshell, the wiring is old and in pretty bad shape, way below code. Using it would be inviting trouble. For safety's sake, I shut if off."

In other words, for now she would remain homeless. Deanna had never been so scared. Want to or not she was stuck at the hotel, wasting her hard-earned money on a room for God knew how long. Knowing she wouldn't have to pay until she received her next paycheck was scant relief.

She gave a miserable nod. Shivering—partly from the cold and partly out of fear—where would she live? —she crossed her arms and tucked her ice-cold hands under her arms.

"That parka isn't warm enough. Here." He started to remove his jacket.

"The label says it's good down to zero degrees," she assured him, compressing her lips to keep her teeth from chattering.

"I want to run something by you. Sit with me in the CRV while I tell you about it."

Curious, she climbed into the black leather seat. He seemed to like the color and it suited him. He started the car and in no time the heater blasted warmth through the car.

"I don't know why I didn't think of this in the lounge last night," he said. "I know where you can live at least temporarily. It's small and basic but clean and snug."

Hardly daring to hope, Deanna pivoted in the seat. "Where is it, and when can I see it?"

"I'll take you over there right now."

Wary, she eyed him. "Where exactly is this mysterious place?"

"About fifteen miles south of here—a couple miles from the station. At my house."

If he thought for one second she'd remotely consider moving in with him after a few steamy kisses... "I don't know you that well, Hank," she said. "And don't forget my rule."

"Eight dates—I remember." His lips twitched. "FYI, even as attracted to you as I am, I don't move that fast." Her face burned and she knew she was blushing. "You'll be on my property but in your own dwelling," he added.

"A guest house?"

Hank shook his head. "A year ago I bought a brand-new, sixteen-foot Scamp—a trailer camper with a bathroom, kitchen, and beds. I'm on a quarter acre of land. She sits on the far side of the yard."

"'She?'" Deanna asked.

"I've always thought of the Scamp as a she."

Deanna couldn't help smiling. "My hatchback is also a she. This CRV is definitely a he."

"I'll buy that."

His grin was wicked sexy. Suddenly, she felt breathless.

Oblivious of his effect on her, he went on. "Refilling the water tank and charging the battery is easy —I'll teach you how."

A gust of wind buffeted the car and swept heavy clouds across the sun. The air darkened, making the morning seem like dusk, and raindrops pelted the windows and roof of the CRV.

For some reason, sitting together in Hank's car felt intimate and romantic. Deanna almost laughed. She really needed to get out more. "Look at this rain."

"Good thing we're in the car. Anyway, with my camping trip canceled I don't plan to use the Scamp until spring at the earliest. I know you prefer to stay close to the hotel, but if you want to move in until you find something to rent, she's yours."

Astounded, Deanna gaped at him. "You're offering to let me live in your camper until I find an apartment," she repeated, to make sure she'd heard correctly.

"That's right."

"Do you make the same offer to everyone who loses a home with no place to go?"

"You're the first and only. Most people aren't as stubborn as you about tapping the benefit fund."

She was beginning to question her hardheadedness. It would be so easy to give in and apply for assistance... No. She refused to be like her parents, would never start down the slippery slope of relying on handouts.

The rain was coming down hard now, pounding the car as if in solid agreement. "I can't possibly accept."

"Sure you can. All you have to do is flash that pretty smile of yours and say, 'Thanks, Hank. I'll take it.' "

His encouragement and generosity were difficult to resist. Heck, everything about the man charmed her. And there was the crux of the matter. She didn't want to be tempted—not until she knew him a whole lot better.

She didn't trust his reason for offering the camper. If he wanted to get into her panties, there were far easier ways. "I need to think about this," she said.

"Of course. You may as well take a look at it."

That couldn't hurt. "When?"

"Now's good."

"But I have to be at work in an hour."

"This is Sunday morning. Traffic will be light. I'll drop you here at your car in plenty of time."

Hard to argue with that. "Okay, but I'll follow you over so you don't have to drive me all the way back."

"It's pouring and you're already in the CRV," he pointed out as he switched on the wipers. "Buckle up."

THE DOWNPOUR REDUCED visibility and made for slow driving. As Hank navigated Kirkdale Road, Deanna stared straight ahead, her hands locked in her lap and her thumbs tapping each other nonstop. Talk about tense.

"The storm makes you nervous," he guessed.

"Not at all." She swiveled her head toward him. "As a rule, men aren't this generous without a reason."

She had that right, but this wasn't about sex. Hank needed to ease his conscience. He ought to tell her that he was responsible for the ash-heap that had been her bungalow, but that window had come and gone last night. Thing was, with or without guilt he wanted to do this for her.

"There you go again, sticking me with motives I don't have," he replied, pinning his gaze to the road. Liar. "You're looking for a place to stay and the Scamp is available. End of story."

At a stop sign he chanced a look at her. And caught her staring at him. Her gaze quickly dropped, but not before he saw soft, trusting light in her eyes. Trust he didn't deserve. The weight on his guilt grew heavier.

Tell me about Froggy," he said.

Deanna's eyes widened as if she couldn't believe he'd asked. "You really want to know?"

"Yeah."

"He sat on the desk of my eighth-grade teacher, Mrs. Steen. The goofy grin on his face made him look friendly. I was struggling in school, barely keeping my head above water. Mrs. Steen was going to retire at the end of the year. She could have ignored me, but she wanted me to make it through high school and go to college. She spent a lot of time tutoring me.

"After each tutoring session she had me explain what I learned to Froggy. That way she knew whether I understood the lesson. Thanks to her, I finished the year near the top of my class. She was so proud of me." Deanna smiled as if remembering.

"As a good-bye gift she gave me Froggy. By then I was used to talking to him. The habit continued, and he saw me through a lot of hard times." She paused. "This will sound silly, but now that he's gone it feels like I lost a good friend."

"That's not silly at all. Why did you have such a rough time?"

"Because a few weeks before I started school, my mom found out my dad was sleeping with his patent attorney's secretary."

Hank could only imagined the upheaval that had caused. "Ouch. He had a patent attorney, huh?"

"He's an inventor."

"No kidding. Has he invented anything I might know about?"

"A few little devices that never earned much. He was always working on something that would make us rich. He still is. They fought day and night. I hid in my room."

"Nasty," he said. "No brothers or sisters to commiserate with?"

"I'm an only child. My mom finally kicked him out."

Hank's parents had their faults, but they'd always been devoted to each other. If they'd split up, he'd have been devastated. "The separation must have been rough on you," he said.

Deanna looked thoughtful. "Yes and no. My father spent all his time inventing things instead of working at a paying job. My mom scrambled to pay the bills but never stuck with any job for long. When you're a child longing for stability and you deal with the opposite day in and day out... Life with them was never easy."

"I'm getting the picture now."

"I sided with my mother for kicking him out. My dad and his girlfriend found a place in Medford and moved in together. It's only twelve miles from Guff's Lake, an easy commute for her. Two years later, when I was sixteen, my mom also decided to leave Guff's Lake. She moved to Corvallis to start fresh, but I wanted to graduate from high school with my friends. I refused to leave."

"What did your mom do?"

"Let me stay. I didn't give her a choice. By then I had a weekend job at Bird's Nest Inn—a B&B across town. The woman who owned it had become a friend, and when I explained my situation and asked for advice she offered me room and board in exchange for doing extra chores. It worked out great."

Both a teacher and a former employer had taken Deanna under their wings, which said a lot about her. Now Hank wanted to do the same thing. He shook his head. "I could never have been on my own at sixteen."

"I did what I had to. I was supposed to join my mother after I graduated but I never did. She was okay with that—by then she and my father had reconciled and Dad had moved to Corvallis." As if imparting a secret Deanna used her hand to cover one side of her mouth. "The other woman is still in his life. She even followed him to Corvallis."

"No way. Does your mom know?"

"Yes, and she doesn't like it anymore than she did before. But she says she loves him too much to kick him out again and looks the other way."

Deanna raised her chin in what Hank had come to recognize as a mixture of pride and determination. "It's my rotten luck to have inherited her faulty judgment in men, but the similarities between us stop there. I will never, ever cling to anyone who puts me second, no matter how much I love him."

Strong and sure of herself and stubborn as hell—talk about a handful of woman. Hank never met anyone like her. "You're something else," he said.

"Is that good or bad?"

"Good." And trouble if he didn't stay away from her.

Yet here he was, offering her the use of his camper.

"This is a nice area," she commented.

"I like it." Abruptly the rain stopped—and just in time. He signaled. "We're almost there. My street is that cul-de-sac up ahead."

10

Because Hank had rented his home before he'd bought it, Deanna had pictured an aging place similar to the older cottages along the street. Not this sleek, rambler-style home and double garage. "Your house looks almost new," she commented as he pulled up a blacktop drive.

"Thanks to a lot of hard work. You should have seen it eighteen months ago."

As he parked beside the garage he nodded at the waving gray-haired man and dark-haired woman next door. The couple climbed into their sedan and drove away.

"You don't use the garage," Deanna noted.

"Not for the CRV. I turned it into a shop for messy home projects."

"That's handy. Appliance repair, your house—I get the feeling you can fix almost anything. I'd like to be able to do that. Did you take classes at the hardware store?"

"Now and then, but I learned most of what I know from Mrs. Chambers. She looked after Hudson and me when our parents were out saving animals."

"Saving animals?"

"They're animal rights activists. Their work takes them all over the world."

Deanna was impressed. "I've never known anyone who did that. How exciting!"

"They seem to enjoy it. Mrs. Chambers was a do-it-yourselfer. She taught us everything she knew and over time we got real good at repairing pretty much anything. We only called a professional when we had to."

"At our house it was the opposite. If something broke it stayed that way. I never even realized it was possible to repair a broken item until I moved into the Bird's Nest Inn."

Hank looked startled. "You waste a lot of stuff that way. The Scamp is over there. Excuse the yard—I haven't had time to rake the leaves."

He directed her toward the far side of the garage, where his camper sat near a six-foot-high privacy fence.

After the downpour the ground was wet and soggy —terrible for her new work pumps. Should've brought sneakers.

Reaching around her, Hank unlocked the door to the camper and opened it. So close that she could lean back against his solid chest... Tempted to do just that, she quickly made use of the welcome mat and stepped inside.

The camper was as small and tidy as Hank had described, and had a cozy feel even without pictures or personal touches. But then he only used it for camping.

A small stove, refrigerator, and kitchen sink filled the front end, with a tiny bathroom along one side. In the back was a dinette table and padded benches with room enough to seat four. There were even storage drawers and a small closet.

The only thing missing was a bed. "I don't see a place to sleep," she said.

"You have two choices, a single bed in the back where you see the storage drawers. They're hinged and make into a bed. Then there's a double in there." He nodded at the table.

"You expect me to sleep on that." She frowned.

His eyes twinkled. "It'd be pretty uncomfortable that way. Watch and learn." With little effort he quickly converted the table and benches into a double bed. "You turn it back into a table."

He stepped aside, providing guidance only when she required it. Within moments she accomplished the task.

"It's a lot easier than it looks," she said. "What a cool place."

"Told you." He raised his eyebrows as in, "Well?"

She needed a place to stay until she found a more permanent home. But to be indebted to Hank in this way seemed too much, and living in his yard... Way too close. How would she keep her distance, let alone ever pay him back?

Unfortunately, at the moment this was her best option. Her only option besides the hotel. Could she make it work?

With opposite work schedules she probably wouldn't see much of Hank. That seemed safe enough. And if she paid her way... "If you're okay with me renting on a weekly basis, I'll take it," she said.

"Who said anything about rent?" Hank frowned. "I don't want your money. You need it for other things."

True, but she had her rules. "I can't stay here unless you let me pay," she insisted.

"Sure you can."

"But I won't."

They locked eyes until Hank swore softly. "You don't back down, do you?"

"Rarely." She named a price she could afford that was less expensive than the hotel but seemed fair.

He countered. She countered back. Finally he rolled his eyes. "I give—we have a deal."

"Wonderful." Smiling, she extended her arm to shake hands. His grip was firm and solid, and for reasons she didn't understand she wanted to hold on. Did, for a little too long.

Heat flared in his eyes, and the urge to kiss him returned.

But that would be dangerous and Deanna wanted safe. She dropped her hand and averted her eyes.

Hank cleared his throat. "When do you want to move in?"

"I'm off tomorrow. Is that too soon?"

"Not at all. I'll be at the station so you'll have to let yourself in."

After he gave her the key she checked her watch. "I need to get going or I'll be late."

On the return drive they worked out where she would park and other logistics before lapsing into silence punctuated with bursts of small talk—the picture of two people comfortable in each other's company.

But the whole way back the electricity between them crackled.

~

"DEANNA'S MOVING INTO THE SCAMP," Hank announced over breakfast at the station Monday.

Max's eyes widened. "How'd you work that?"

"She needs a place to stay until she finds an apartment. My camper isn't going anyplace, so why not?"

He recalled her initial refusal to consider the camper and her change of heart when she saw it. She was so easy to read that he'd known she wanted it before she told him.

He also knew she wanted him. Likewise. In bed last night he'd laid awake and imagined her under him, calling his name as he satisfied her...

Damn, he was doing it again now. He forced the arousing images from his mind. Sex with her was not in his future.

Across the table, Tony shook his head. "Couldn't find anyone to camp with on your week off—that's a crying shame."

"No prob—I figured out another way to fill the time."

"Day hikes around the area?" Rafe asked.

"Maybe, but I'll fill the bulk of my time working on Oliver's—Deanna's bed & breakfast."

Captain Comings narrowed Hank a look. "She's staying at your camper and you're going to use your vacation to help her out. You're still blaming yourself for what happened."

Partly, but Hank's feelings had evolved into something more. "As I said the other day, I really want to help her," he said, refusing to look away from the captain's assessing look. He did not need therapy.

The corner of Max's mouth lifted. "You sly dog—you're into her."

No point in denying the truth to the guys who knew him so well. "Doesn't mean I plan to do anything about it," he assured his smirking crewmates.

"Why not?" Max asked. "You're single, she's single…"

"She just lost everything." Thanks to him. "You know how it is with me and women. I'm not the right man for her."

Tony gave a sage nod. "She could use some stability in her life."

That, and Hank didn't want to be responsible for adding any more disappointment to her life than he already had. "Exactly."

The captain's eyes narrowed further. "You charging her rent?"

"Yeah." Never mind that Deanna had demanded it.

"Correct answer." With that, the captain relaxed.

"What'll you do with the money?" Max asked.

"Donate it to the benefit fund."

"Back to Oliver's," Rafe said. "What kind of work are you thinking?" He owned a fair amount of rental property and had done a fair amount of carpentry and remodeling.

Hank had given the matter some thought. "For starters, updating the wiring. I did an inspection the other day. The circuit breaker is as old and dangerous as the bungalow's was. I shut the power off."

"You're not qualified to do a big job like that," Rafe pointed out. "No one in the room is, including me."

"Got it covered—I'll get her to hire Jory Rader. He'll let me do the grunt work, which will save her a bundle."

Max eyed him. "And Deanna, who won't tap our benefit fund and I'm guessing insisted on paying rent, is okay with that."

"Haven't told her yet." Around the table, guys shook their heads. "Look, I didn't work any of this out until the wee hours this morning. God's honest truth, I'll phone her as soon as I get a minute to myself."

The conversation moved on, crewmates sharing how they'd spent the weekend. Hank tuned out. Telling Deanna he wanted to work on her bed & breakfast was sure to be a bumpy conversation. She'd probably fight his decision, damn her misplaced pride.

The captain collected his breakfast remains and stood. "See you in ten at the morning meeting."

"You should have joined us at Lucky Joe's Saturday night," Max commented as he and Hank disposed of their trash en route to the apparatus bay on the lower level. "Lots of fine women on the dance floor."

Hank had spent the evening with his own fine woman. She's not mine, he reminded himself. She never would be.

All the same, he wanted her.

11

____

The one benefit of losing almost everything was that packing didn't take long. Deanna's possessions fit easily into the hatchback. After checking out of the hotel and stopping for groceries and a drive-thru for a mocha, she headed to her temporary quarters.

It wasn't an ideal place or location, but having a temporary place to call home was a definite step forward. She couldn't help but feel thankful and optimistic.

Having missed the morning rush and in no hurry she drove at a leisurely pace, enjoying the blue sky and October sunlight that seemed to smile on the brilliant autumn leaves.

In Hank's driveway, she admired the contrast of the beige shutters, closed up tight against navy siding. Since she'd been here yesterday he'd raked the yard, stuffing leaves into fat, plastic bags piled against the garage.

Curious, she walked around the entire perimeter of his property.

The yard was huge and the grass still green. Scattered trees, but no bushes or flower beds. Just a brick patio with a covered barbecue grill. It needed a gardener—or a woman's touch.

Once Deanna had read an article that said the state of a person's home reflected the state of their mind. She wondered whether the inside of Hank's house was as neat and clean as the outside, and whether it also lacked the little touches that made a house into a home. Not that it was any of her business.

With the shutters and drapes pulled across every window she had no way of peeking in. She did note that the large picture window facing the back was sparkling clean.

She finished her stroll and returned to her hatchback. Next door, the sedan from yesterday pulled into the driveway. The same couple exited. Setting down their purchases, they ambled toward Deanna, their faces lit with curiosity.

"Hello," the woman called out, the color of her coal-black hair obviously from a bottle. "If you're looking for Hank, he isn't home."

"Yes, I know—he's at work."

The man's comb-over didn't quite hide his receding hairline. "Something we can help you with?" he asked.

Deanna flashed her "Welcome to our hotel" smile. "I'm Deanna Oliver. I'll be staying in the camper for a while."

"The camper?" The man shook his head. "That's a new one."

His wife elbowed him. "I apologize for my husband. We're the Blocks—Carolyn and Otto."

Otto smoothed his comb-over. "What I meant was, Hank's lady friends usually stay at the house."

"You don't know that, Otto. Hank is a very private man. We have no idea about his love life." With a sly gleam in her eyes, Carolyn leaned toward Deanna. "I do know that he loves that camper and that you're the first woman to stay there."

Oh, dear God, the woman assumed Deanna and Hank were together. Deanna set her straight. "It's not what you think—Hank and I are friends." Or something. Deanna wasn't sure what. "I'm having trouble finding an apartment and I needed a place to stay."

"Of course you do," Carolyn crooned in obvious disbelief. "Welcome to the neighborhood, Deanna. If you need anything at all, just knock on our door."

"I will. Thanks."

Silently laughing, Deanna unlocked the camper. Without Hank's big body looming nearby, the tiny space felt roomier. And a bit lonesome, but Deanna wasn't about to go there. More light would help. She opened the curtains. Like an old friend, sunshine poured in a cheerful welcome.

Much better. Humming, she returned to the car and began to carry her things inside.

Unpacking didn't take long. In short time her few clothes had been neatly folded into storage drawers or hung in the closet, and her shoes arranged in a tidy row on the floor. Her scant remaining possessions—assorted magazines and paperback books, phone and laptop, an alarm clock, and the crocheted afghan Bea had given her after the fire—added a personal touch that made the camper feel more like a home.

For as long as she stayed here. In the near future, she hoped to move into something more permanent. But for now, the pressure of finding an apartment had eased. For the first time since the fire she could breathe again.

~

After brewing a pot of coffee in the camper's coffeemaker Deanna sat down at the surprisingly comfortable bench at the table and called Vi. "Can you talk?" she said by way of greeting.

"Until the phone rings or someone walks in. It's pretty slow right now. What am I saying? This is the off season—we're dead in here. I haven't heard from you in days. How are you?"

"Doing well." Deanna gave a silent salute to her snug little home.

"That can only mean you rented an apartment. Hooray!"

"I wish but I do have a place to live until I find one."

"Let me guess—the hotel lowered its rates for you."

"Very funny. Hank offered me his camper."

"That was fast. Last time we talked you said he wasn't interested."

Which she'd believed until Saturday night. She wasn't ready to share what had happened just yet. "Everyone knows I'm stressed about where I'm going to live. Hank is helping me out until I find something —that's all," she explained. "I'm paying rent."

"He's charging you to stay in his camper?" Vi sounded indignant.

"He didn't want to, but I refused to stay here otherwise."

"I should have guessed. It wouldn't hurt you to let a guy do something nice for you now and then."

"I did. After work Saturday, I met him for drinks."

"You and Hank Gardener had a date?"

"It wasn't a date. He ate at the Hearthstone—he wanted to check that I was okay." Even saying the words, Deanna felt warm inside. "We chatted a bit.

When my shift ended we decided to meet at the lounge."

"I'm liking the sound of this."

"Dream on, but except for a kiss or two nothing happened."

"Nothing? You and Hank kissed. Hold on while I fan myself. And?"

"He's good at it." Understatement of the year.

"Mm, I can just imagine. Are you going to stick to your eight-date rule before you get physical?"

"Of course," Deanna assured her friend with more certainty than she felt.

"One down, seven to go."

"Eight. I'm not counting Saturday night as a date."

"Why not?"

"He didn't exactly ask me out. The lounge is so close to the lobby that it seemed natural to continue our conversation there."

"In my book, that qualifies as a date. When do I get to see this camper Hank is loaning you?"

"Renting me," Deanna corrected. "I'm here now. I moved in this morning. Why don't you drop by on your way to work tomorrow? Hank lives fairly close to the station, not too far from the visitors and convention bureau."

"You didn't mention that the camper is at his place. This gets more and more intriguing."

"Believe me, it isn't. I work on his days off and he works on mine. I doubt we'll see much of each other." For her own good Deanna counted on that.

"Trust me, if the man is interested in you he'll figure out a way. What's his house like?"

"I haven't been inside, but the outside is neat and well-kept. He's in a pretty neighborhood on a cul-de-sac."

"Maybe he'll invite you in sometime. Any word from the insurance company about money and when to expect it?"

Deanna had already filled Vi in about the reduced compensation she was due. "No, but I suspect researching what building materials cost fifty years ago takes time. I'll let you know when I hear from Matt. Meanwhile, I'll do what I can at the B&B and continue to look for an apartment."

"Heck, if I were standing in your shoes, I'd forget about that and concentrate on other things. Namely Hank Gardener."

Already Deanna was way too focused on him. "It's time I checked listings online and tackled the rest of my to-do list," she said. "I'll let you go."

"In other words, we're not going to talk about Hank anymore. All right, but—" Vi cut herself off and lowered her voice. "Someone just walked in. Text me with updates."

Deanna disconnected and opened her laptop.

12

An hour later Deanna texted Vi. Found a surveyor. Meeting the trash hauler 2 clear away the fire mess & seeing 2 apartments.

Think you're crazy 2 look but gd luck, her friend replied.

Deanna was almost at the apartment complex of the first appointment when the manager alerted her that the unit had been rented. Heaving a weary sigh, she made a U-turn and headed for the second complex a mile or so up the road.

The GPS directed her to turn but she missed the street and had to circle the block. On the way she spotted a weathered, six-story clapboard. Out front, a woman was staking a For Rent sign into the ground.

Deanna braked to a stop and rolled down the window. "How many bedrooms in the unit, and what's the rent?"

The woman quoted her a sum she could afford. "It's a furnished studio."

Not too expensive and she wouldn't have to buy furniture? Hardly believing her good luck, she sucked in a breath. "May I see it now?"

The woman led her inside. The unit was on the

ground floor. Although old, it seemed in good condition and wasn't too expensive—perfect.

"I'll take it," she said. "When can I move in?"

"The current tenant will be out November fifth. We'll need a day to clean. Will the seventh work for you?"

"Absolutely." There and then Deanna signed a six-month lease and paid the deposit. Pleased and relieved she wouldn't have to use Hank's camper for long, she smiled all the way to her property, where she'd set up a meeting with Ed, the trash hauler.

She was early and Ed hadn't arrived yet, which gave her time to tell Hank about the apartment. Not wanting to bother him with a phone call during work, she texted and asked him to call when he could. She would share the good news then.

DURING A LULL LATE MONDAY AFTERNOON, Hank ducked into the tiny room where he bunked at the station. Sitting on the edge of his tightly tucked bed, he checked in with Deanna. "Got your text. All moved in?"

"Yes, and I'm so glad you called."

Liking the sound of that, he grinned. Then sobered. There was nothing between them and never could be. She deserved a better man. "Any problems with the camper?"

"None so far. I didn't expect to find a coffeemaker in the cabinet. Now I have all the creature comforts I need. Things are definitely looking up. You're the best!"

She sounded happy. Knowing he played a role in that felt good. "My pleasure."

He was about to tell her his idea to work on her bed & breakfast when she added, "This camper is only part of the reason for my great day. I found a surveyor."

"Way to go."

"There's more. I was on my way to look at an apartment today when I got lost. That's how I found a furnished studio that hadn't been listed yet. The location is perfect—halfway between your house and the resort. I signed a six-month lease."

"Huh." So much for helping her with her living situation. Hank chalked up his major disappointment to the fact that she was leaving before she'd had half a chance to settle in at the camper. "When do you move?"

"November seventh."

Three weeks from now. The tight feeling in his chest eased. "You still need a place to stay for several weeks."

"That's right. I just finished a late lunch and I'm still at the table, all cozy and warm. Have I mentioned how much I like it here?"

Hank chuckled. And wished he was there with her so that she could thank him in person. In a very physical way.

"If you think the bench and table is comfy, wait till you try out the bed," he said.

Bed and Deanna. His body revved into overdrive. The catch in her breath further catapulted his fantasies. He pictured her, naked and hungry on the mattress, her blond hair spread across the pillow...

Way too turned on, he stood and began to pace, not easy in the room's limited space. "I always sleep great in that bed," he added.

Although with Deanna beside him, sleep would be the last thing on his mind...

In the brief pause that followed, he imagined she shared similar fantasies.

She tumbled into a new subject. "I met Ed, the trash hauler. He quoted me an excellent price and he happens to have an opening this Friday. He said to tell you hi and thanks for the referral. Thanks from me also."

"Any time. You've been busy today. But then, that's how you roll."

"You're the same way. How's your day so far?"

Hank returned to the bed and sat down, using the wall as a backrest. "We've been busy, too. So far a compost silo that spontaneously combusted, a call to rescue a little girl from a claw machine, and a false alarm."

"What's a claw machine?"

"A machine with toys inside. You put money in and work a claw to pick up a toy. They're all over the place. "

"How in the world did a little girl get in there?"

"On a dare from her sister, she crawled into the prize chute to get a toy she wanted. She couldn't get out. They're both grounded. It'll be on the evening news."

"That I have to see. I'll make sure to tune in." Deanna snorted. "You handle some very interesting situations."

"Tell me about it. We have our downtime, too. Like now. I hope it lasts. I need time to bone up on material for a training class tomorrow."

Studying wasn't required, but Hank intended to hit the books anyway.

"You take classes?"

"A couple times a month. It's a requirement of the job. We teach, too. Max will lead tomorrow's workshop."

"What's the subject?" she asked.

"How to read smoke."

"Reading smoke," she repeated, sounding puzzled. "How does a person do that?"

Did he really want to talk about this with her? No, but thanks to mentioning the class he was stuck. Way to go, bozo.

His good mood evaporating, Hank thunked his head against the wall, then stood and resumed pacing. "Reading smoke takes practice and skill. It's an important tool that helps us determine when a fire is about to escalate. We can then act accordingly to minimize danger to other firefighters and damage to the structure."

Unless someone, in this case, him, effed up. He exhaled loudly.

"Is something wrong?" Deanna asked.

Damned if he'd admit to feeling like hell. "As I said, there's a lot of reading to do before tomorrow morning."

"Don't worry, you'll get it done," she said, misinterpreting his brusque tone as study anxiety. "I almost forgot to mention that my insurance agent called about an hour ago. My reimbursement check will be about a tenth of what I expected, but it should arrive in a few days. I'm ready to line up bids for wiring. Can you recommend someone?"

Talk about a great lead-in for what he wanted to say. "I know a great guy for the job. By the way, I figured out how to spend my vacation next week."

"Let me guess—you need the camper."

"Nothing like that. It's yours until you move. I want to work on Oliver's."

"That doesn't sound like much of a vacation. You're supposed to get away from work, remember?"

"I don't consider renovation work. I enjoy taking part in a building's transformation. If I didn't, I would've hired someone to make the improvements on my own place."

"Oliver's belongs to me, Hank, and it's my responsibility. You say your house isn't finished. Why don't you finish it instead?"

Scowling, he flicked a speck of lint off his pants. "I figured you'd fight me on this."

"Then I—"

Sick of her misplaced pride, he cut her off. "Just listen, okay? The guy I mentioned? His name is Jory. He's an electrical engineering wizard and I recommend him all the time. I already lined him up to do the job. We're meeting at Oliver's Wednesday morning so that he can see what's what. The following Monday he'll do the job."

"You set this up without asking me first?"

"Look, Jory usually books weeks in advance and I wanted to save time. I pulled a few strings to get you on the schedule."

"How much is it going to cost me?" she asked, sounding wary.

"We won't know until Jory assesses the situation, but it'll be less than you think. He owes me for all the business I send his way. Plus I agreed to help. He'll cut you a nice price break."

"Oh, Hank, I don't know..."

Man, she frustrated him. "You're too smart to be this foolish, Deanna. This is a good deal. Take it."

She went quiet, then sighed. "What time Wednesday are you meeting him?"

"Eleven. You'll be at work but he'll call and let you know the details."

"You'll need the key again," she said. "I'll leave it under your kitchen door mat."

Relieved she'd quit fighting him, Hank stopped moving and canted his hips against his closed door. "That won't work—I won't go home until after the meeting."

"Then I'll hide it at Oliver's, on the ledge above the front door. Tell Jory I'll be joining you to assist."

Seriously? Hank frowned. "You don't have to help. I suspect most of what I'll be doing will be in the cold, dirty crawl space behind the basement."

"I want to know how it's done. Dirt is no problem —I'm washable and so is my parka."

Hank marveled over the fact that she actually wanted to get her hands dirty. Suddenly the alarm sounded, quickly followed by a message from dispatcher Sarah McCone.

"What's that?" Deanna asked.

"Fire call. Gotta run."

Hank disconnected, raced toward the brass pole down the hall, and slid down to the apparatus bay.

13

"This camper is adorable," Vi said when she stopped by on her way to work Tuesday morning.

"I don't know that Hank would approve of your description, but it fits. Do you have time for coffee? I made a fresh pot." Deanna gestured at the table, where she'd set out mugs, sugar, and milk.

"Sure. I could use another cup."

Seated on the bench, Vi looked around. "You have a kitchen, a bathroom, and a cool place to sleep, and Hank is a few dozen yards away. Are you positive you wouldn't rather stay here?"

"I can't, not indefinitely—that isn't the deal I made with Hank," Deanna said. "I need a place where I can stay for a while. Besides, the apartment is closer to the resort. And don't forget, I prepaid first and last month rent and signed a lease. Can I ask you something?"

"Of course."

"Am I making a mistake, letting Hank work on Oliver's?"

"He offered to do that?"

Deanna nodded. "He had scheduled a vacation for next week. Then his plans fell through but he still has to take the time off. He claims to like renovating and offered to help with mine. He knows what he's doing, too—he did most of the work on his house."

"Maybe he'll take you on a tour and point out the changes. I sure like the look of the exterior." Mug clasped to her chest, Vi gave released a sigh of admiration. "I see no problem with him working on the B&B. I say let the man do whatever he wants and I don't just mean renovations. If he's interested in you, you'd be crazy not to date him."

"He hasn't exactly asked me out. I haven't even seen him since he handed over the key to this camper."

"Duh—he's working forty-eight hours straight."

"True, but we've been in contact by phone. He could have brought it up then." Although the conversation had been interrupted by a fire alarm.

"Maybe his idea of dating is different from yours."

"Come on, a date is a date. A man calls, he asks me out, and we go somewhere."

"Not necessarily. Hanging out is a kind of date, like you and Hank did in the lounge that night he kissed you. But if you prefer the more formal route, what's stopping you from taking the initiative?"

"No way," Deanna said. "That'd be too much like chasing after him." Something her mom would do. "Even if he asked, I'm not sure I'd go."

Vi groaned. "It's been over a year since you and Rusty broke up, way past time to move on." Deanna opened her mouth, but her friend plowed ahead. "If you don't get to know Hank better, how will you find out whether you're meant for each other?"

"You're such a romantic. I'm not." Believing in happy endings had only set her up for pain and heartache. "We were talking about Hank and the renovations at Oliver's. How much am I supposed to pay him?"

"Did he mention money?"

"No, but I have to compensate him. It's only fair."

"I agree. Bake cookies or make him a meal."

"I'm talking about cash. And have you forgotten what a bad cook I am?"

"How could I?" Vi laughed. "Your mac and cheese —ugh."

"Tasteless and mushy. I know. And don't forget my infamous roast chicken."

"Burned on the outside and raw inside." Vi wrinkled her nose. "Maybe cooking isn't such a great idea. Treat him to dinner or bring in takeout."

"Too much like a date."

"Can't you get a package of premade cookie dough?" Vi said.

Not a bad idea. Deanna could pick some up today and bake the cookies tomorrow night. That way they'd be good and fresh when she gave them to Hank on her way to work Wednesday morning. "I don't remember seeing a cookie sheet in here, but I'll bet I can borrow one from Carolyn next door," she mused.

"There you go."

"I still need to know how much to pay him."

"Ask him what he charges."

"He'll tell me to smile and say thank-you."

"Then call General Hardware. The people there are bound know the going rate for renovation work."

Soon after Vi left, Deanna drove to the supermarket and bought chocolate chip cookie dough. When she returned she headed to Carolyn's to borrow a cookie sheet.

She wouldn't mention who the cookies were for. No point fanning the fires of the woman's misguided imagination. Hank hadn't indicated he wanted to date her, and there was little indication he would.

~

As HANK and his crewmates filed out of the training room Tuesday, Max signaled for him to hold up. "You didn't like my workshop," he commented.

Hank frowned. "Where'd you get that idea? My brain is reeling from all your great info."

"You knew most of it."

"I should have."

"Next time you'll be better prepared," Max said. "I know I will—even if I have been at this thirteen years. Prepping for the class and teaching was a good refresher for me as well. Now I'm hungry. Lucky thing it's almost lunchtime."

A whole group of Hank's buds ambled to the bathroom to wash up.

"This is your last day before you officially start your vacation," Rafe commented over the hiss of the water at the sink. "What's on your agenda for tomorrow?"

"Breakfast at Rosemary's and a stop at the store to get some food before I meet Jory Rader at Oliver's. He'll assess the funky wiring situation and I'll find out what my job will entail."

"Deanna okayed your plan to help her out, huh? Smart woman."

"Yeah, and get this—she asked to help with the grunt work. Surprised the hell out of me."

Rafe seemed taken aback. "Doesn't she trust you to do the job?"

"Could be, seeing as her ex lied about it before. Jory's a licensed pro and he's sure to check my work. I doubt this is about trust. It's more about wanting hands-on experience."

"Cool. I don't know many women interested in that. Jill sure isn't. She loves to get her hands dirty when she's making her pretty pottery, but hang out in a dark, musty crawl space? No way."

"That job won't take more than a day or two," Max commented as he dried his hands. "What then?"

"The siding damaged during the fire needs to be replaced. I'll tackle that. I can't do the windows—she'll need to hire someone for that—but I do know my way around installing drywall."

"For all those walls? That's a huge job, buddy. If you wait until next weekend, I'll give you a hand."

"Count me in," Tony offered.

"I'll be there, too," Nate said.

Hank flashed a grateful smile. "A week from Saturday it is."

"Maybe once you do all that work on Deanna's B&B you'll finally clear your guilty conscience—misguided as it is," Max said as they tromped up the stairs toward the kitchen.

"That isn't my only reason and you know it," Hank replied for what felt like the dozenth time. "I want to help her out."

A few steps ahead, Rafe glanced back at him. "You don't have to explain. Deanna's beautiful, she's independent, and she's single. Hell, if I were single I'd be doing the same thing."

Hank snorted. "Don't you guys ever listen? I'm not going there."

The snickers and leering grins pissed him off. He flipped his crewmates the bird, entered the kitchen, and headed for the fridge to retrieve his lunch.

14

———

Deanna was sound asleep, dreaming of chocolate chip cookies and Hank, when a knock at the door startled her awake.

Thinking she was in the bungalow she burrowed under the covers and muttered, "Go away."

The knock sounded again. She opened her eyes and realized she was in Hank's camper.

It was eight-thirty a.m.—later than her normal wakeup time, but after a late night baking cookies she'd slept in.

"Deanna?" Hank called out. "You in there?"

"Give me a minute."

Scrambling up, she hurried into the bathroom, where she did her business, brushed her teeth, and ran a brush through her hair. Much better. On the way to the door, she shouldered into her robe and tied the sash.

Hank stood on the step, one arm propped against the doorjamb. The pose, his faded jeans, and the black I hate being sexy but I'm a firefighter so I can't help it T-shirt stretched across his gorgeous chest made him irresistible. He looked clean and alert—the opposite of her.

He raised his eyebrows. "I woke you. I thought sure you'd be up."

"I didn't get to bed until late and decided to sleep in." Cold air rushed through the door, making her shiver. He wasn't even wearing a jacket. "Come inside before we both freeze," she said.

Inviting him into his own camper felt strange. As soon as he wiped his feet and entered she shut the door.

"I brought your key back."

Deanna put it in the pocket of her robe. "I won't be coherent until I get my caffeine," she said. "Would you like coffee?"

"Sounds good."

While she started the coffeemaker Hank leaned against the counter, not far from the foil-covered paper plate of cookies.

He lifted the foil and sniffed appreciatively. "Chocolate chip cookies."

"They're for you for meeting with Jory and getting me a good price. He called yesterday with his estimate. The cost is as reasonable as you said."

"I like this payoff." The grin lighting his face trans- formed him from handsome to out-of-this-world gor- geous. He popped a cookie into his mouth. "These are delicious. Did you bake them in the camper oven? I've never used it."

"Works great. You do realize it's barely eight-thirty in the morning. How can you eat a cookie at this hour?"

"I've been up for a while."

He helped her convert the bed into the table and benches.

"I realize you're an early riser, but this is Thursday," she said. "You could have slept in."

"I wanted to get my run in before my first appliance repair appointment at ten."

She opened the curtains and caught him checking out the backs of her bare legs. Thrills raced up her spine. His slow, knowing smile made her wonder if he'd somehow read her thoughts.

"You're barefoot," he said.

With toenails in bad need of fresh polish. She curled them against the vinyl cork floor. "I haven't replaced my slippers yet. Did you go ten miles?"

He nodded. "A long run on a cold, clear morning is the best."

"And here I am, barely awake." The coffeemaker gave a loud gurgle and fell silent, beeped, and fell silent.

Hank set the cookies between them while Deanna placed mugs, the coffee pot, milk, and sugar within reach. They sat down across from each other. Hank's knees didn't touch hers under the table, but all the same she felt his warmth.

Deanna scooted as far back as the seat allowed and busied herself with her mug. Dealing with her attraction to Hank before she'd had one sip of coffee was no fun. She regretted inviting him in.

"I like your hair loose around your shoulders," he said.

The warmly uttered compliment both pleased her and made her self-conscious. Anchoring her hair behind her ears, she filled him in on the latest. "Jory's going to replace the electric panel and replace or repair some, but not all the wiring. The rest is okay."

"That's great."

"He also says it's good that many of the walls are down to the studs, because access will be easier, which will save time. He calculates one to two days to get the job done. He gave me the okay to help, but says the decision is up to you."

"I'm cool with it." Hank helped himself to another cookie. "Don't make me eat these alone."

"It's too early. I haven't even had breakfast."

"Make cookies your breakfast today."

Having sampled quite a bit of dough the night before, Deanna should have had her fill. She certainly didn't need the sugar high. But chocolate was one of her biggest weaknesses. That and Hank's encouraging grin sapped her willpower.

Halfway through a cookie, she smiled. "I see your point—these make a great first meal of the day. But they're supposed to be for you."

"Maybe I like to share."

After polishing off the whole thing, she licked her lips to get all the chocolate. Caught him staring at her mouth and switched to a napkin. "I know I look terrible."

"You're wrong." His hot gaze flickered over her, as if she was the cookie he wanted.

Despite her tingling private parts she managed a frown. "Straight out of bed, without any makeup? Come on."

"I'm serious. Your skin is lightly flushed and your eyes look extra blue in the morning light. There aren't a lot of women who can pull that off naturally."

Spoken like a man who knew what he was talking about. How many women had he woken up beside? Deanna didn't want to know and refused to become another notch on his belt. "I borrowed a cookie sheet from your neighbor, Carolyn. She and Otto assume we're sleeping together."

"Where'd they get that idea?"

Deanna feigned indifference. "Maybe from all the women who've spent the night at your house."

"I can't remember the last time that happened. Way before I bought the place, and not often." He hooted. "Those two need to find hobbies."

"They do seem on the nosy side. To be clear, I'm not interested in jumping into bed with you."

"Then you'd best fix that." He nodded at her chest with smoldering eyes. "You have no idea what that does to me."

She looked down to where her robe had gaped open. Despite the thick, oversize T-shirt she slept in, she could see the points of her nipples. She jerked the lapels together. "I didn't do that on purpose. This is a second-hand robe. The hook is broken and I don't have a needle or thread."

She let out an embarrassed laugh. "Even if I did, I don't know how to sew. I don't have any safety pins, either. I keep forgetting to buy them. I need to add them to my to-do list."

Realizing she was babbling, she sucked in a breath. "You should go."

His lips twitched and he glanced at his lap. "I need a minute."

He was turned on, just as any guy would be. All the same, Deanna's traitorous body began to hum. The urge to throw herself at his mercy and indulge in the pleasure they both wanted was almost too strong to fight.

Remember the eight-date rule, the logical part of her mind insisted—and just in time. Reining in her desire, she slid from the bench, collected the mugs, and deposited them in the sink.

Hank also stood. "Thanks for the coffee and treats."

"You're welcome." She replaced the foil and handed him the plate.

Without taking his eyes from hers he returned it to the table. "Be careful, Deanna."

Had her collar come loose again? She glanced down. Nope. Confused, she squinted at him. "What do you mean?"

"Your hair."

"What's wrong with it?"

"It swishes when you move. A guy can't help but wonder if it's as soft as it looks." He lifted a lock and let it fall through his fingers. "Feels like silk." His eyelids lowered to half-mast and his voice sounded hoarse. "Smells good, too. You smell good. I want your scent all over me."

With every honeyed word her composure slipped until her lips parted on a soft sigh.

Hank groaned. "You'd tempt a saint, and God knows I'm far from that."

He reached for her. A tremor shuddered through her, shredding the remnants of her self-control. She stepped willingly into his welcoming heat.

DEANNA WAS soft and warm and eager. In sweet need she clung to Hank. Hungry for her taste, he coaxed her lips apart and slid his tongue into her mouth.

He untied her robe and cupped her breasts. Moaning, she arched up into his palms. She hooked her leg around his thigh, settling in nice and close.

Sweet jeezus, he wanted her. Almost bad enough to forget that he always disappointed the people he cared about, and that thanks to his mistakes, she no longer had a home.

But not quite.

Breathing hard, he tore his mouth from hers and unwrapped her leg. He straightened her T-shirt and retied the robe, hiding the nipples that had frayed his control.

Her eyelids fluttered open. Hunger had darkened the blue to a bewitching smoky gray. Her mussed hair, kiss-swollen lips, and the flush of desire staining her skin seduced him all over again.

Through sheer strength of will he backed away. "I need to get out of here while I still can."

He strode outside, shutting the door firmly behind him.

15

Dazed, Deanna sank onto the bench Hank had vacated. He'd been so anxious to leave that he'd forgotten the cookies. Refusing to call him back, she considered setting the plate at his front door as she left for work. But she couldn't risk the possibility of facing him again.

Not with her body aching for him, all her female parts alive and primed for more. After a year without a man she shouldn't be surprised. But she was upset.

What had she been thinking, inviting Hank inside when she liked him way too much for her own good? They hadn't even had a real date, let alone eight. A rule she'd devised to protect herself. Yet intoxicated and seduced by Hank's desire, she'd thrown caution to the winds and behaved like the love-starved woman she was.

His eager mouth, his hands loving her breasts... Biting the pad of her thumb, she crossed her legs— and banged her knee on the underside of the table.

"Ouch!" she cried.

Why hadn't that happened when Hank was seated across from her? The pain might have helped her get a grip on herself.

The alarm on her cell phone buzzed—her morning wakeup call. That, too, might have snapped her out of her fog of desire.

Probably not.

She rose and rifled through the closet for work clothes. The shower's warm spray sluiced over her nipples which, thanks to Hank's clever attention, seemed extra sensitive. The wetness between her legs had to do more with her desire than the water.

Afraid of emptying the camper's water tank she quickly finished. Within minutes she was dressed. Foundation and mascara did wonders for her looks— no matter what Hank said. Last of all, she brushed the hair he liked so much and tied it back.

Fully clothed and groomed, she looked her normal self, professional and in control. No outward signs that she'd been thoroughly kissed and aroused to within an inch of losing her mind.

She'd been so hot that if Hank hadn't stopped they'd be in bed right now...

Her longing moan filled the camper.

What was the matter with her? She didn't need this desire, couldn't afford the distraction. Especially with Hank. He'd advised her to stay away. His neighbor's comments, whether exaggerated or not, had underscored his words. If she was smart she'd heed the warning.

The safety of her heart depended on it.

~

FOR A WEEKNIGHT MARV'S was hopping, just as Hank had figured it would be. Country western music spilled from the diner's old juke box, all but drowned out by laughter, conversation, and the clatter of dishes.

Aside from good burgers and great beer, the restaurant was a great place to meet women. Tonight Hank counted on that. He needed the distraction from Deanna.

Everything about her and this morning had blown him away, to the point that he could think about little else. As bad as he wanted to get naked with her and finish what they'd started, he couldn't let that happen.

He checked for possibilities. A pair of attractive females sat at the bar, sipping beer and looking around. The one with the dark hair gave him a flirty smile.

She was curvy and attractive—exactly what he had in mind. Ambling over, he nodded at the stool beside her. "Is this seat taken?"

"It is now." Her smile widened. "I know you—you're Mr. May."

"That's me." Calling him "Mr. May" was a dead giveaway they'd never met. He slid onto the stool. "I'm Hank."

"Bobbie." She gestured at her friend. "This is Paula."

From behind the bar, the bartender headed over. Hank ordered a beer and burger for himself and cocktail refills for his new lady friends.

As soon as the drinks arrived Paula excused herself, took her drink, and moved somewhere else.

Hank and Bobbie started talking—or Bobbie did. He couldn't get a word in. The shrill laugh punctuating her non-stop chatter got old fast. Before long and with zero encouragement, she ran her palms down his chest, placed her hands on his thigh, and got all up in his face. She'd really caked on the makeup and perfume, he noticed.

Why had he considered her attractive?

He preferred a different type of woman, straightforward and able to listen as well as talk. Like Deanna. Her makeup was understated and she smelled nicer. She didn't laugh often but when she did she meant it.

He regretted ever sitting down. When his food arrived he ate fast, then made a show of checking his watch. "I need to be somewhere."

"So soon?" Bobbie pulled a pout. "Let me give you my number."

"That's okay. You have a good night." He handed the bartender a bill. "Keep the change."

On the way to the car he shook his head. Attempting to push Deanna from his thoughts had done the opposite. He only wanted her more.

Too bad he'd run that morning, because he sure needed to clear his head. While the car idled he searched his cell phone for a movie at the local theaters. Nothing interested him. The bowling alley, then. He hadn't played in a while.

Halfway there he changed his mind and instead headed home to watch the tube and call it an early night.

16

Ready to let down and put her feet up after work, Deanna turned into Hank's driveway. The CRV was gone, and a good thing. After a long day, her aching desire for him had faded. She had her feelings safely under wraps and intended to keep them that way. Best not to see him.

Naturally, the instant the thought formed the man pulled in. The mere sight of the CRV headlights gave her heart flutters, and the unwanted heat she'd banished rushed through her.

So much for avoiding the man. She might not be ready to face him but as a strong, capable woman she could handle this. Keep herself in line and stay calm.

Hank slid out the driver's side. The motion detector lights that had shuddered on bathed him in bright, artificial light and cast long shadows behind him. His stride smooth and easy, he headed toward her. Powerful, lean, and muscled...

For all her talk of self-control, she failed to stem a sigh of admiration.

Why did he have to be so darned gorgeous?

She masked her attraction under a neutral smile

and hugged her purse—as if it could shield her from his magnetic pull.

"Hey," he said, his breath fogging in the cold night air.

She'd zipped her parka all the way up and her slacks were comfortably loose. Yet his gaze heated as if she were dressed in skintight clothes, whipping every cell in her body into frenzy of longing.

Her resolve skittered to a halt. Until he moved in closer. The overpowering smell of cheap perfume emanating from him shocked her. But she had no hold on Hank. They weren't even dating. He had every right to be with any woman he chose.

It was just... This morning he'd seemed so into her.

He'd lost interest already, while the heat from his kisses and caresses burned hot in her. Men.

"How was your day?" he asked.

She stepped back. "Long."

"Mine, too. I left those chocolate chip cookies at your place this morning," he said with a gruff edge to his voice. "I sure would like some."

The desire on his face made it clear he was talking about more than cookies.

With total disregard for the perfume all over him, her most female parts began to thrum. No, thank you. "I'll get them. Wait here."

By the time she returned she was fuming and determined to forget what had happened this morning. To forget she liked Hank, period. He was just a guy letting her stay in his camper.

"Here." She thrust the plate at him.

He looked startled. "You're mad at me."

Ya think? Deanna widened her eyes.

"Because of what happened in the camper? You enjoyed that as much as I did."

His dark eyes glittering, he fingered a lock of her hair just as he had before his first kiss this morning. God help her, she trembled.

"Right or wrong I want more with you, Deanna."

He sounded sincere. But like all the men she'd cared about, he said what she needed to hear, then did as he pleased without any concern for her feelings.

She jerked away, forcing him to drop his hand, and crossed her arms. "I'm not some naïve girl, so don't expect your hungry looks and sweet talk to sway me. It's obvious you've been with a woman tonight."

He frowned, then snorted. "You mean Bobbie? I can explain."

"Don't bother. Just... Stop looking at me like I matter when I don't."

"Oh, you matter."

There went his eyes, frank and warm. Deanna started to melt when he added, "But I'm all wrong for you."

That she believed. Totally. In her mind, anyway. If only her heart and body were on board.

"It's true that at Marv's tonight I sat next to this woman at the bar—Bobbie," he went on. "Before long and with no encouragement on my part she was all over me. That's why I smell like carnival cotton candy." He made a sound of disgust. "I split and drove straight here."

His met her eyes squarely. Either he was a skilled liar or he was telling the truth. Her instincts told her to go with the latter, but her judgment had failed her too many times.

Deanna wrinkled her nose. "You really need a shower."

"That and to wash these clothes. Are you still mad?"

Not with him, only at herself for starting to care too much. She shook her head.

Hank exhaled loudly as if he'd been holding breath. "Go get some rest."

"I will. Good night."

As she crossed the driveway she stole a look at him. He hadn't moved. The light wreathed him in melancholy shadow, this potent, solitary male keeping watch as she made her way toward the camper.

She wasn't used to anyone looking out for her and certainly didn't need that now, not in Hank's own backyard.

All the same, knowing he was there gave her a warm, secure feeling she welcomed—even if she didn't understand it.

~

AFTER A PREDAWN RUN in the sleeting rain, Hank returned home wet, cold, hungry, and unhappy. For the first time in his life, the distance and breath-stealing pace had failed to clear his head.

Blame it on Deanna. He hadn't been thinking straight since the day at Rosemary's. Kissing her hadn't helped.

The corker? Thinking he'd pick up a woman at Marv's and forget her when he was already too far gone.

One glimpse of her in the driveway last night and he'd been eager to pull her inside for more. Of all the lamebrain, knucklehead things... She had that effect on him, making him forget what was right and going after what he wanted instead. And he wanted her like he'd never wanted a woman.

Planting his feet on the mat inside the kitchen

door, he removed his sodden gloves and windbreaker. Then his muddy shoes and socks.

A decent man would tell her the truth, admit that he was responsible for the loss of her home. Hank couldn't do it because he couldn't bear to lose her respect and admiration.

Didn't that prove his parents right—again.

Want to or not, memories pulled him straight back to the day that had destroyed what little hope they had for him. The details as fresh as if it had happened yesterday.

They'd gone shopping for an upcoming trip to Africa, leaving Hudson and him at home. Hudson's friends had come over and they'd hung out in his room with the door closed. Hank went outside to toss a ball with kids from the neighborhood.

In his eagerness to join them he'd forgotten to click the back door shut behind him, when he knew Cayenne, their red setter, would work it open and bolt. An eight-year-old kid shouldn't be so careless.

Hank and Hudson had combed the neighborhood and the adjoining woods in a fruitless search to find the family dog.

Telling his parents had been one of the worst moments of his life. Losing the family dog was punishment enough. Hank had also been banished to his parents' permanent shit list.

To this day they didn't think much of him. Not that it mattered anymore. He'd given up trying to gain their respect long ago.

The respect and trust of his crewmates made up for that in spades, and most of the time he managed to feel okay about himself and forget who he was deep down. But with this fire disaster and his foul-up hammering him in the gut... Kind of hard to circumvent that.

Filled with self-loathing, he kicked the kitchen trash can. Not smart in bare feet and ice-cold toes. Damn that hurt. With a satisfying screech the can skittered across the tile.

Then it smacked against the stove and tipped over. The lid popped open and coffee grounds and trash spewed everywhere. Muttering, Hank limped over, righted the thing, and cleaned up the mess.

Ten minutes later he'd eliminated all signs of his hissy fit. Too bad he couldn't clean up his mistakes as easily.

But he could steer clear of Deanna. He wished he hadn't given her the okay to help him with the wiring next week. Nothing he could do about that now except stay cool, keep his hands to himself and quit fantasizing about her.

Yeah, that'd work.

In a much better mood, he stripped, lobbed his running clothes into the laundry hamper, and padded to the shower.

17

For some reason the Hearthstone was unusually busy all weekend. Deanna had worked later than usual and hadn't seen or spoken with Hank since the night he'd reeked of perfume. She hadn't exactly gone looking for him, either.

She'd hoped that steering clear of him and constantly reminding herself that her mind was in charge and she needed to slow way down would help.

No such luck. She liked and wanted him more than ever.

She didn't have a clue how he felt, but en route to Oliver's Monday morning he seemed to be as ill at ease as she was. The relentless rain and slick roads weren't exactly mood relaxers, either.

And here they were, about to spend an entire day working together. They needed to get along. Determined to lighten the tension, she made small talk. "What a nasty day to be out."

Hank's grim nod wasn't friendly and relaxed, but anything was better than a blank expression.

"If you think driving in this stuff is bad, try running," he replied.

"You didn't."

"Yep."

"There are indoor tracks around here, you know."

"I use them when it snows. Otherwise, I prefer the great outdoors."

She gave him a sideways look. "I don't know whether you're crazy nuts or crazy disciplined."

To her relief he almost cracked a smile. "Both."

"At least we'll be inside all day," she said.

Without heat or electricity. The very thought her feel cold. "I'm looking forward to learning tons," she added, to remind herself why she'd volunteered to help. "By the way, I stopped by to see Bea before work Friday. When I mentioned what we were doing today she promised to stop by around lunchtime with treats."

"Sweet—pun intended." Another half-smile.

Hank parked near the bed & breakfast. Intermittent hard rain had washed away the tire tracks from the trash hauler truck but not the gaping hole where her home had once sat. The construction on the bungalow had been so slapdash, it didn't even have a concrete foundation. No wonder it hadn't stood a chance of surviving the fire.

Gone in a flash. Deanna swallowed past the lump in her throat.

"Ed did a great job cleaning up over there," Hank commented.

She agreed. "Except for the large indentation in the ground, you'd never know my little oasis used to be here."

Hank's bland look seemed at odds with his terse nod and sudden grip on the steering wheel. He'd gone tense again.

"I set up an appointment with the surveyor I contacted," she added. "We'll meet here Saturday, during my lunch break."

"You'll probably get a decent chunk of change for it, but I recommend filling in that hole first. Although maybe not, because whoever buys it may want a hole to lay the foundation."

"I'd rather fill it," Deanna mused. "All I need is a pile of dirt. Any suggestions?"

"Ideally you want someone looking to get rid of a load. Let me check with Rafe. He's done extensive work on his rental properties and can probably come up with a name."

"I'd appreciate that. I don't know what I'd without your help," she said. Then shut her mouth.

She didn't want Hank to think she was beginning to rely on him. She wasn't. The only person she could count on without fail was herself.

Jory, a barrel-chested, middle-aged man about five feet ten, stood under the overhang sheltering the front porch of Oliver's with two employees. Surrounded by various tools, stepladders, and other supplies, they greeted Deanna and Hank with ready smiles.

Hank pulled off his gloves and shook hands with everyone. Jory followed suit with Deanna. She unlocked the door. The four men hefted equipment and followed her inside.

As she'd suspected, the interior was almost as cold as outside. She blew on her cold hands and rubbed them together. "Too bad we can't turn on the furnace or use a space heater."

Hank frowned. "I thought you were going to get yourself new gloves."

"Eventually. I've been kinda busy lately. It doesn't

matter—I won't be able to wear them while we work, anyway."

He set down his gear and handed her his well-worn leather gloves. "Until then, wear mine."

She shook her head. "You need them. Besides, they're way too big."

"Put them on," he ordered.

"Yes, sir. Ooh, fleece-lined," she murmured, nearly swooning with pleasure. They smelled like him, too.

Jory had made a schematic of the house and wiring. While his assistants tromped around the main floor and upstairs to scout out the situation, he, Deanna, and Hank headed to the basement.

With Jory's flashlight lighting the way, they descended the well-worn basement stairs, their steps accompanied by the wood's groans and creaks.

"Without the overhead light, it's kind of spooky down here," Deanna said.

Jory nodded. "This would be a great haunted house for Halloween. Do you get many trick-or-treaters at your place, Hank?" he asked as they made their way across the concrete floor to the far side of the basement.

"When I'm home. Halloween falls on Friday this year, and I'll be waiting. I expect around fifty kids."

"That's a lot—almost as many as we get at the hotel," Deanna said.

A week later she'd move into the apartment she'd rented. Now that she'd adjusted to the camper she had mixed feelings about that. Staying another month or so would have been nice. She was comfortable there and liked knowing Hank was nearby—even if her feelings for him were dangerous. Safer to live someplace else, away from him and the constant temptation he presented.

"We all wear costumes to work," she said.

"So does my wife," Jory commented. "She works at a dentist's office and is planning to dress as the tooth fairy. What are you going to be?"

Deanna hadn't had time to think much about that. "I don't know yet. Something easy."

"I still have the firefighter's shirt and hat from when I earned my degree in fire science," Hank said. "You're welcome to borrow them."

"That'd be interesting. Let me think about it." The shirt would probably swim on her, but—

A cobweb caught her in the face. "Ew!" she shrieked and ran straight for Hank.

"Easy there." He dropped his things and caught hold of her upper arms. After an assessing gaze he picked a string of the sticky webbing from her hair. His eyes twinkled. "You tangled with an old spider web and won."

Jory had pivoted toward her, his bushy eyebrows raised. "You won't see spiders this time of year. It's way too cold."

"Thank goodness for that." Deanna was mortified at her behavior. Now they'd think letting her help was a mistake. "I don't like spiders," she admitted. "Or their webs."

"So we noticed."

Hank chuckled low in his throat, a contagious sound. She couldn't help but smile in return, which reduced her embarrassment.

"There are sure to be old webs in the crawl space," he said. "Last chance to back out. You're welcome to take my car and go someplace warm. I'll text when we finish and you can come pick me up."

As tempted as Deanna was to do just that, she raised her chin. "I'm staying right here."

She made a silent vow not to be so skittish next time.

After climbing a stepladder and removing the cover that concealed the crawlspace from view, Jory glanced at Hank over his shoulder. "Hand me the other stepladder and I'll set it up in there. Once I hang the battery-powered lanterns you follow me in. Deanna, you'll go last."

Hank nodded.

"I'll spend most of the day down here with you two," Jory added, "but at times I'll leave to check on my guys."

In no time Hank lifted Deanna from the ladder onto the packed dirt ground. His hands stayed on her waist a split second longer than necessary. Heat flashed in his eyes and her body responded in kind.

At the same instant they turned away from each other to await Jory's instructions.

~

"We're done here." Jory brushed his hands together and then threw Hank and Deanna a thumbs-up. "Thanks to my crew and you two, we finished in a day."

Relieved that the job was over, Hank looked forward to a hearty meal and getting warm. Deanna had returned his gloves long ago, but the work they'd done had prevented him from wearing them. With the exception of a few short breaks and lunch fueled by Bea's fresh coffee and cake, they'd been at it almost ten hours. In the damp cold.

"A very long day," Deanna said. "But who's complaining? We did it—yay!—and I didn't even freak out when I stepped into that other spider web. Not much, anyway. Knuckle bump." Wearing a proud grin, she fist-bumped him and Jory.

She was so pleased with herself. Hank felt pretty damn good about that. Even better, concentrating on work had taken his mind off his attraction to Deanna to the point that his libido had gone AWOL.

No sexual vibe from her, either. She'd focused one hundred percent on the work at hand. Not a single complaint about the at-times challenging work or the less-than-comfortable conditions, either. She'd impressed the hell out of him.

And bonus: For the first time since they'd met she seemed completely at ease, revealing sides of herself he hadn't witnessed before. She had a great sense of humor. He'd laughed more today than he had in a long time.

"You did good," he said as she reached the stepladder out of the crawl space.

"Real good." Jory studied her with respect. "You're a hard worker and a fast learner. If you're looking to get into this line of work, give me a call."

Her eyes widened. "You're kidding."

"I don't joke about my livelihood."

"I'm flattered, but as soon as I fix up this place I'll be opening for business. Oliver's Bed & Breakfast— your home away from home."

"Catchy phrase," Jory said. "I like that."

Upstairs, Deanna stood under the blazing overhead light in the vestibule and wrote out a check. Jory handed her a receipt and wished her luck with her endeavor. While she locked up, Hank helped carry tools and equipment to the man's truck.

It had grown dark outside. The rain had stopped hours earlier and the temperature had fallen. Shivering visibly, hands in her jacket pockets, Deanna met him at the CRV.

In the CRV he cranked up the heat and she settled back in her seat.

"I can't believe how comfortable I feel around you now," she said as the tires crunched over the gravel drive. "I guess because we worked together."

Hank nodded. "We make a good team."

"We do, don't we?" Her smile lit up the dark car. "Will you let me help you replace siding tomorrow?"

A task that could easily be done solo. But she was in such high spirits... "If you don't mind being outside all day. It'll be colder than it was in the crawl space and could rain again. Also, I'm planning to pick up the siding materials around eight-thirty. That means leaving the house at eight."

"For a chance to learn more, I don't mind."

Hank shook his head. "Trust me, it's not that exciting."

"It is to me." She rubbed her hands together, reminding him of a kid anticipating her birthday.

He laughed. "All right, then."

"I wish I could help with the drywall, too. Are you sure you want to spend even more of your time on that?"

"Yep."

"I'm going to pay you for your time."

He didn't want her money or an argument and decided that along with the rent he'd add whatever she paid him to the benefit fund. "Suit yourself," he said.

"Thanks—I will. Did I mention that I'm meeting the window guy and the insulation people before work Wednesday? The insulation goes in Thursday and the windows on Friday."

"Good to know, as I'll be putting up drywall Friday. Things are really moving along."

"Finally." Her stomach growled.

"Someone sounds hungry," he teased.

"Someone is."

"You're not the only one. I'm so empty I could eat a mountain." After their day together and the newfound camaraderie between them, it seemed natural to share dinner. "Let's get something to eat on the way home," he suggested.

"I would, but..." She gestured at her filthy coat and jeans. "I can't go into a restaurant looking like this."

"That's why God invented takeout. Name your preference—Mexican, Chinese, Thai, burgers?"

"They all sound good, but I'd kill for a pizza."

Deanna on a food rampage—that'd be something to see. Hank grinned. "Don't want you doing that. Pizza it is. Harvey's?"

"Is there anyplace else?"

She smacked her lips and his grin rolled into a chuckle. "A woman after my own heart. Harvey's is always hopping. You'd best call ahead. Get an extra large."

"Great idea." She pulled her cell phone from her jacket pocket. "By the way, I'm buying. After saving me a bundle of money today and teaching me so much that's the least I can do. Besides, you paid that time at the lounge. It's my turn."

No point arguing about that, either. "Okay."

"Hey, would you like to see the renovations I made on the house?" he asked when she disconnected.

"I would love that."

Her enthusiasm was something special. Too bad she couldn't bottle the stuff. She'd make millions.

"Then it's settled—we'll eat at my place," he said. "After dinner I'll give you the grand tour."

For the remainder of the drive to Harvey's and the whole way to the house they alternated between banter and silence, as peaceful as if they'd known each other for years.

Hank congratulated himself on keeping his attraction tamped way down. As long as he didn't touch her or think about kissing that tempting mouth—and he wouldn't—everything would be fine.

18

"As hungry as I am, I really need to shower and change clothes," Deanna announced as Hank pulled up the driveway. "Would you mind holding dinner for a little while?"

Hank had been thinking along similar lines. "No prob—I'll do the same. When you're ready, come over."

As they exited the car, headlights from an approaching vehicle flashed them. The driver honked and Hank raised his hand in greeting. "That's Carolyn and Otto."

"Hi," Deanna called out, waving.

"Now that they've seen us together they'll be talking."

"Let them. I'll be back soon."

In the house, Hank set the oven on low. He maneuvered the large pie onto a pizza pan, sliding it into the oven to keep warm. Whistling, he headed to the bathroom to shower and dress. By the time Deanna showed up he'd set the table.

She arrived in loose jeans and a turtleneck sweater. "It's freezing out there," she said, breathless.

"What happened to your parka?"

"It took all of twenty seconds to run over here. Besides, that jacket is so filthy I couldn't put it back on. When we finish tomorrow I'll take it to the Laundromat."

With her hair clean and almost brushing her shoulders and her face free of makeup, she looked much as she had the other morning—both sweet and sexy.

Hank's chest swelled with feelings he didn't understand. He barely contained the urge to reach out and run his fingers through those silky locks until her eyes darkened and glazed with desire.

He wanted to make her his in the most primal way.

And he'd thought he'd corralled his attraction to her. Wrong. He shoved his hands in his jeans pockets and backed up a healthy distance.

Deanna was too busy looking around and sniffing the air to notice. "I always dreamed of a kitchen like this, with enough room for a big table." With a playful smile she leaned in and lowered her voice as if about to confide something private. "But at the moment all I care about is our pizza. It smells amazing."

His good humor restored, Hank bowed. "Yes, ma'am, coming right up. Grab something to drink and make yourself at home." He gestured at the beer and soda he'd set on the counter.

The pizza was piping hot. He placed the pan within easy reach of them both, then sat across the table.

After helping themselves they dug in and conversation ground to a halt. Deanna's moans over the food filled the room. If she did this with pizza, Hank could only imagine what she sounded like during sex.

She licked tomato sauce from her thumb and the

fly of his jeans got a little tight. He was real glad for the napkin on his lap.

The right move would be to get her out of here as soon as the meal ended. But he'd promised to show her the house.

Everything about her turned him on. How in hell was he supposed to keep his hands off her? He almost groaned in frustration.

He would keep his focus on dinner and the tour, period, give her a quick look around, and hustle her out.

Good plan—as long as he stuck to it. For both their sakes, he hoped to God he did.

~

HANK NODDED at the pizza box. "One more slice left. Help yourself."

Full to bursting she shook her head. "After what I just put away? You finish it."

"I'm saving room for dessert."

He was just mentioning that now? "If you'd have said something earlier, I wouldn't have had seconds. There's no space left in my stomach—I can't eat another bite." Seconds later, unable to resist the allure of something sweet, she eyed him. "What have you got?"

"Oreo cookies."

Only her favorites ever. "I guess I could force one down," she said.

His lips quirked. "Atta girl. Sit tight—I'll be right back."

He strode across the room to the pantry, still lean and mean despite consuming a huge quantity of the pizza. A hottie and a patient teacher willing to explain the hows and whys of wiring. He'd also loaned her his gloves.

Was it any wonder she liked him more than ever? Which would have been dangerous if they both weren't so comfortable and relaxed.

Unopened package of cookies in hand, Hank returned. "Got 'em."

"Be still, my heart."

He laughed. "I knew you had good taste. What's the grin for?"

"When you laugh I can't help but smile. I've smiled a lot today."

"What can I say—you crack me up."

He thought she was funny? "That's a new one."

"Trust me, you are. I can't eat Oreos without milk. You?"

"Is there any other way?"

"Again, we're on the same page." He grinned. "You get the milk, I'll get the bowls."

"Bowls?"

"To dunk the cookies. A glass is too small."

"What a cool idea. I don't know many people who like to dunk cookies in milk," she commented a few bites later. "At least, not in a bowl."

"You've been hanging with the wrong crowd."

He reached for a new sleeve of Oreos, but she shook her head. "This time I mean it—I really am full."

"All right. Ready for that tour?"

"Not until we clean up our dinner mess."

"And I thought I was a neat freak. Plates, glasses, and bowls—I'll take care of them later."

"I'd rather tidy up first."

"Were you born with a neatness gene like I was?" he asked as they set the kitchen to rights.

For the first time that evening she didn't feel like smiling. "It evolved as a way to control chaos."

Hank gave a somber nod. "Makes sense. We're all through in here. Follow me."

He led her to the living room, a vast space with an impressive stone fireplace and skylights. "Wow," she said. "This one room is bigger than the studio apartment I rented."

"I knocked out the dining room wall and reduced the attic by half. This is what it used to look like." He pulled out his phone and showed her several images.

Deanna studied the before pictures. "This doesn't even look like the same house. What you've done is amazing."

His chest puffed with pride. "It wasn't all me. Rafe and some of the other guys helped. Take a look at these."

He called up photos of the old windows, standing close to point out differences. Not touching her, but near enough that she felt the warmth from his body and smelled his clean scent. Suddenly she could barely focus. "The new windows make a huge difference," she managed.

As she moved aside Hank pocketed his phone. His bicep brushed her breast. Her nipples sharpened and the dangerous feelings she'd repressed flooded back— an aching desire to pick up where they'd left off and the sweetness that came from caring about him far more than was wise.

Heat flared in his eyes and they both glanced away. He cleared his throat. "Excuse me."

For her own good she ought to go. But leaving in the middle of the house tour seemed rude. Deep down, she wanted to be right where she was.

I can't trust my judgment, she reminded herself.

For all the good that did. Her aroused body continued to hunger and thrum.

"Um, what's next?" she asked in an effort to get her mind back on topic.

"The half bath." He gestured to the adjacent door, which was closed. "When I bought this place it didn't exist."

Curious, she frowned. "What was here before?"

"Wasted space—a useless closet." This time he handed over his phone and stood out of reach. "That was then. This is now." He opened the bathroom door.

She'd looked at enough bathroom materials to recognize the Italian tile on the floor and counter. "It's beautiful, Hank. You did this yourself?"

"Everything but the plumbing."

"I'd love to be able to do my own tile."

"It's not as hard as it looks."

He didn't offer to teach her, which given her feelings was a relief.

"Maybe General Hardware offers a class," she said.

"If not, they'll create one for you." He nodded at the room across the hall. "That's my office."

Deanna stuck her head inside. Shelves and files, a gorgeous wooden desk straight out of a decorator magazine, and the usual computer and printer. She wanted an office like this. Someday.

Next, he showed her a guest room, and finally, the master suite.

Slightly unnerved she stood in the threshold of this most intimate and private part of his home. She took little note of the scattered paintings on the walls. Her gaze fixed on the bed. Clean lines, dark wood, with a no-nonsense, masculine quilt, it filled half the space. A man his size needed a big bed.

How many women had he shared it with? Deanna

didn't even want to think about that. It was none of her business and a timely reminder to push her feelings for him way down deep where they wouldn't work against her.

"Anything wrong?" Hank asked, standing at her shoulder.

Yes—she wanted him. "I'm taking it all in. I'll bet this used to be two rooms."

"That's right. I've torn down a lot of walls in this house. After you."

"I don't need to go in." She stepped back, smack into his chest. His broad, very solid chest.

She knew she should move away but her legs refused to cooperate. From behind he wrapped his arms around her. Helpless against her overwhelming desire, she sank against him.

19

"This is a bad idea," Hank warned, fighting to control the terrible hunger burning through him. Despite his words, his arms stayed right where they were—wrapped around her. He couldn't have moved away to save his life.

Deanna shifted slightly, her soft rear end against his groin. His brain fogged up. He nuzzled her neck. "Your hair smells great."

"Honey and vanilla scented shampoo." She bent her head to one side, baring the sensitive crook of her neck.

Hank brushed the smooth skin with his mouth. Shivering, she leaned her full weight into him and brought his hands to her breasts. "Touch me."

He cupped her, squeezed gently, and teased her nipples with his thumbs. Her breath caught.

Turning her to face him, he ravished her lips. She tasted even better than before and was just as eager. He couldn't get enough, wanted to love every part of her.

Dangerously close to the point of no return he tore his mouth from hers. "We shouldn't do this. I'm not the right man for—"

"Stop trying to talk me out of what we both ache for."

"I don't want you regretting anything later. What about your eight-date rule?"

She blinked. "We spent the entire day working together in a dim, damp crawl space. That's worth at least six dates. Then we had dinner together. That makes seven. If you count drinks and nachos in the hotel bar, we're at eight."

"You said the lounge thing wasn't a date."

"I changed my mind." She licked his throat. "Quit arguing and kiss me again."

Lost in her soft skin, her curves, her vanilla and woman scents, he sank to the floor, bringing her with him. She climbed onto his lap, straddling him. Hard and throbbing he ground against her most feminine part.

At some point she inched back. "Take your shirt off."

He removed it. "Now you."

Her eyes hazy and slightly unfocused she tugged her sweater over her head, revealing a plain beige bra. The center front contained a tiny gold key. Intrigued, he ran his finger over it. "What's that for?"

"It's the clasp."

"Cute." He unhooked the thing and tossed the bra aside, exposing small breasts and rosy, upturned nipples rigid with desire. "Sweet God in heaven, you're beautiful."

Playing with both breasts at the same time, he made her squirm, arousing them both. At some point, she replaced his hands with her own.

"Put your mouth on me," she whispered, lifting her breasts in an offering he couldn't refuse.

He got busy. Before long, she squeezed him with her thighs. He grinned. "I think you like this."

"Mm."

"And this?" He nipped and suckled.

A funny little catch in her breath, then a longing moan. "Please don't stop."

He laid her down and slid his palm over her ribcage and stomach, straight to the button on her jeans. "I'm going to make you come," he growled, undoing it.

When she didn't object, he tugged the zipper down. Then he was inside her panties and entering her with his fingers. She was wet and wild against his hand. He'd barely begun before she shuddered and climaxed.

"That was fast," he said, pleased.

"I couldn't help myself."

A red flush tinted her fair skin, and her hair went every which way. Hank would have sold his soul to be buried inside her but he'd already taken her further than he'd intended.

He sat up and pulled her with him. She turned her back to dress. Giving her extra privacy, he averted his head and donned his shirt.

Fully clothed, he pushed to his feet and offered Deanna a hand up. She was awful quiet.

"Hey." With his fist he nudged her chin up. "Everything okay?"

She nodded. "I don't know about you, though." Her gaze darted to his erection.

"Don't worry about that. I enjoyed myself. A lot."

He walked her to the door and kissed her gently. "See you in the morning."

Leaning against the doorjamb he watched her run through the cold toward the camper.

And wondered what the hell they'd started.

FOR A LONG TIME after Deanna left, Hank sat in the living room in his favorite easy chair, nursed a beer, and stared at the empty fireplace. A roaring fire would have been nice but he hadn't had time to make one earlier.

Not that he'd needed it. He and Deanna had generated their own heat in what ranked as one of the hottest evenings of his life.

Christ, what had he been thinking? Thinking? He barked a laugh. Around her his good intentions took a back seat to sexual desire. What red-blooded male could resist her long legs, sweet ass, and perfect breasts? A guy would have to be half-dead not to be tempted.

Her passionate response had blown him away. Passion being only one of many sides of her that turned him on. Her eagerness to learn the how-tos of wiring and replacing siding—stuff most women cared nothing about. She also made him laugh.

Even more astounding, despite the nasty curve-balls life had thrown her, she refused to give up on her dreams.

Hank shook his head in admiration. Deanna Oliver had attitude and grit in spades. She was one of a kind, a breath of fresh air, and a double shot of smokin' hot. Being with her turned him upside down and inside out so that he didn't know whether he was coming or going.

Once again he'd tried to warn her away, and hadn't that gone well. She wanted him just as bad as he wanted her. Fooling around with her was like playing with matches in a parched meadow—sooner or later she was bound to get burned.

And he'd agreed to bring her along tomorrow?

Bad move.

Nothing he could do about that now except stay out of trouble. Like that had worked so far. Good thing she needed to go to the Laundromat at the end of the day.

In the morning he'd give her an out to stay home and make it clear that what had happened tonight shouldn't have and wouldn't again. If she still wanted to help with the siding, so be it, but at the end of the day they'd go their separate ways.

This time he meant that. Period, over and out.

That settled, he banished Deanna from his thoughts, drained the last of his beer, and then headed for bed.

Yet for all his determination, like an addict he craved more.

20

Prepping for the day ahead, Deanna made ham and cheese sandwiches and enough sliced carrots for her and Hank. They hadn't discussed this, but he'd spent the first day of his vacation working at Oliver's and was about waste more of his precious time today.

Lunch was the least she could offer. Nothing else, though. Not like last night.

She hadn't meant to get carried away, but when his big, brown eyes darkened to the color of melted chocolate because he wanted her, she wanted him back. Voraciously.

Closing her eyes she recalled every kiss, nip, and touch. And caught fire all over again.

Hank was such a great guy, offering her his camper and willing to teach her renovation skills. He'd driven all the way to the Hearthstone to check on her. All without asking for anything in return.

He wouldn't do those things unless he cared about her. Despite his claims to the contrary, he seemed like a good and decent man. She wanted badly to believe that.

Her heart already did, but it had steered her wrong so many times. She was leery of trusting her feelings.

She lowered her head and frowned at her left breast, which concealed her heart. "You are not in charge anymore—got that?" she warned.

Until she knew for sure that Hank was the man she believed him to be, they needed to slow down.

She packed the food into a paper bag and tidied up, wrinkling her nose as she donned the filthy parka and headed outside into a perfect autumn morning— sunshine and cool, crisp air.

Hank was moving tools from the garage to the CRV's open gate, his profile in sharp relief against the blue sky. Straight nose, proud chin, and sensual lips that knew exactly how to make her crazy... There went her insides, all warm and melting.

He caught her staring. "Hey," he greeted, pinning her with an unreadable gaze.

"Good morning," she returned, sounding remarkably unaffected when she could barely form a thought for the wanting inside.

Keeping her distance wouldn't be easy. She needed to mention slowing down as soon as possible. The thought of telling him made her feel more in control.

She held up the paper lunch sack. "I hope you like ham and cheese."

"A lot more than the PB&J I slapped together. You made me a sandwich?"

"We both need to eat. But there is a problem—I'm out of chips and cookies. I had to substitute carrot sticks."

She expected a laugh. Not even a hint of a smile.

He shut the garage door, then pivoted toward her. "Listen, we need to talk."

Apparently she wasn't the only one with that agenda. "I agree."

"You first," he said.

A sudden case of nerves made her stomach contract. What if he lost interest in her?

Was she that insecure? Uh-huh.

Deanna gave herself a mental eye roll. She didn't think he would but if he did, if he moved on... Better to find out now, before she made a huge mistake and fell for him.

His hooded gaze only upped her anxiety. Who knew what he was thinking? She plunged ahead anyway. "I think we moved too fast last night."

"You have regrets—I knew it."

"No. I'm not at all sorry. I enjoyed every second of yesterday and last night— Well, except for the spider web."

"Me, too." Heat shimmered in his eyes before his expression shuttered closed. "Still, it shouldn't have happened. It won't again."

She expected an argument or an attempt to persuade her otherwise, not for him to throw up his hands without a fight. Stunned, she gaped at him. "Who said anything about stopping? All I'm asking is that we slow down."

He started to reply but his ringing cell phone cut him off. He slid the device from his hip pocket. "It's Rafe—I should take this. Hey, buddy. Everything okay?"

He listened, then glanced at Deanna. "She's right here. Hang on." He handed over the phone. "Rafe has the name of a guy with fill dirt for that hole in the ground."

"Great. Hi, Rafe. Thanks for getting back with a name. What am I doing with Hank?" she repeated for

Hank's benefit. "We're about to pick up siding materials at the hardware store. That's me, Deanna the eager assistant. Let me find a piece of paper and something to write with."

She handed Hank the lunch sack and fished through her purse. When she hung up a few minutes later she couldn't help but laugh. "Rafe said I should tell you to be good."

"Smartass." Hank's lips twitched. "It's getting late. Do you still want to help today?"

She nodded. She also wanted to finish the conversation.

"Climb in and buckle up." On the way down the driveway he slanted her a cryptic look. "Before we pick up our supplies, I need to stop at the drugstore."

Double lines of vehicles crowded Kirkdale Road and traffic crept forward at a turtle's pace.

"Damn rush hour," Hank grumbled. "Every year it seems to get worse."

"With my schedule I rarely have to deal with this," Deanna said. "Guff's Lake sure has grown."

"Along with an upsurge in medical and fire calls."

"I hadn't thought about that."

When they finally reached the drugstore, Hank pulled into a parking slot. "Need anything?" When Deanna shook her head he opened his door. "I'll leave the car running so you don't freeze."

While he was gone she turned on the radio and wished Rafe had called at a different time. The abrupt end to her conversation with Hank had left her unsettled. She needed to know whether he truly wanted to stop what they'd started. Until then, she doubted she'd draw a deep breath.

～

Armed with a pair of fat plastic sacks and deep in thought, Hank exited the drugstore. He wasn't surprised that Deanna didn't want to stop what they'd started. Neither did he but they had had to.

He found her rocking out to something on the radio. Grinning for the first time today he knocked on her window. She lowered it and the music.

"Here." He handed her the bags.

"What's this?" she asked.

"See for yourself."

By the time he rounded the car and slid into his seat she'd pulled out the jumbo bag of cheese popcorn and the candy bars he'd bought.

"I approve of your taste in junk food." Setting the treats aside, she delved into the other bag. First out—work gloves. Then a burgundy glove and hat set.

"These are really nice. Are they for me?" she asked.

"Yep. You can't work outside in this cold without something to protect your ears and hands. The matching gloves are for when you're not doing repairs or renovations."

"Thanks. How much do I owe you?"

"Nothing. They're a gift. A local women's shelter raising money was selling them at a table inside. They're handmade and washable."

"But—"

"A gift," he repeated. "Better try on the hat before we leave to make sure it fits."

She pulled it over her ears so that the fold-up ribbing reached clear to her eyebrows. "It fits. Thank you."

A split second later she started to tug it off. He'd never seen a woman have so much trouble accepting a gift.

"Not so fast," he said, stopping her.

First he tucked stray locks behind her ears. Her vanilla and honey scent flirted with his senses and he wanted to bury his nose in her hair. Instead, he adjusted the hat to cover her ears, then turned up the ribbed cuff so that most of her forehead was visible. "Much better. Check it out."

Using the mirror attached to the sun visor she cast a critical look at herself. "This is a good color for me. Thank you." This time the words sounded heartfelt.

"You're welcome," he said. "You look cute."

"I'm twenty-eight years old. I don't know that I want to look cute."

"All right, pretty and sexy."

She glanced away and removed the hat, releasing fine, flyaway strands that floated around her face. "We haven't finished our conversation about last night," she said.

Resisting the urge to smooth his hand over her head and tame her hair he rapped his fists against each other. "Sure we did."

"You'd really rather stop than slow down."

Her eyes locked on his. For a moment he lost himself in the blue-gray depths. "I didn't say that."

"You said and I quote, 'It won't happen again.' What if I want the opposite and more?"

"Trust me on this—you don't."

She glared at him. "You do not get to tell me what I do and don't want."

"Not even for your own good?"

She crossed her arms. "Now you sound like a parent. Telling me something is 'for my own good' when you don't have a clue what I need? Step off."

Women. Hank blew out an exasperated breath. "Do you ever listen? I'm. Trying. To protect you," he stated through gritted teeth.

"Puh-lease. I don't need you or anyone else protecting me. I'm perfectly capable of taking care of myself."

Bull-headed seemed a more apt description, but Hank knew better than to say so. He'd never wanted a woman more. Grasping her upper arms, he hauled her as close as he could, right up to the divider between the bucket seats. "So we're clear here, you want me deep inside you—when you're ready."

"Yes."

Her lashes fluttered to half-mast, shooting his hands-off plan to hell. Hank no longer cared.

"Don't say I didn't warn you." He kissed the self-righteousness right out of her. When her soft moan filled his ears he released her. "We good now?"

Wearing the dazed look he'd come to anticipate, she nodded.

"All right. Let's get that siding."

21

After a very long day every cell in Deanna's body dragged with fatigue. She didn't have the energy for a conversation. Judging by Hank's silence, neither did he. As he drove through the dark toward his house neither of them spoke.

But her mind whirled. From start to finish, today had been unlike anything she could have imagined. He'd bought her two pair of gloves and a hat, plied her with cheese popcorn and chocolate bars, and once again warned her away. He'd also spelled out exactly what she wanted, then had kissed her senseless—all before they left the drugstore.

If that wasn't thrill enough, he'd knocked the ball right out of the park by patiently explaining how to replace damaged siding. He'd encouraged her to test her skills, which had lengthened what was probably a half-day job into double that.

This afternoon she'd accidentally sliced her little finger on a razor-sharp cutting tool. Hank had cleaned and bandaged the wound and wrapped her in a big, comforting hug. When she insisted on going back to work, his atta-girl grin had made her feel proud of herself.

All of it proving he was a great guy, the best man she'd ever known. For once her heart had steered her right. As he pulled up the drive she smiled to herself.

"You seem happy," he commented.

"This was another banner day. I learned so much."

"You're a good student."

"Did I earn an A?"

"It would've been an A-plus if you hadn't hurt yourself."

"I promise to be more careful next time. Hey, before I forget, I think I will borrow those old firefighter clothes and hat of yours for Halloween."

"Can't wait to see that. I'll dig them out for you."

"Great." As he turned into his driveway she yawned. "I wish I didn't have to go to the Laundromat later. I could wear my trench coat to work tomorrow, but it's too lightweight for this cold weather."

"That's right—you want to wash that dirty parka. I'm happy to add it to the load I'm doing tonight." He extended his arm.

Too exhausted to argue she slipped it off. "If you end up skipping laundry tonight, don't worry. I'll wear a sweater under the trench."

He leaned across the seat and gave her a quick kiss. "Get some rest."

"You, too."

Warm clear through, she exited the car.

Deanna woke up Wednesday with aches and pains in muscles she hadn't realized she had. Not yet ready to dress for work after her shower, she donned a pair of sweats, grabbed her laptop and sat down gingerly on the unmade bed. Handling the front desk today shouldn't be too bad, but surviving the hectic night at the Hearthstone might pose a challenge.

A knock sounded at the door that could only be Hank. Smiling she stood, pausing as her protesting muscles adjusted to the movement.

She made her way to the door and let him in. "Hi. You're not out running."

"Finished a while ago. Here are the parka and the shirt and hat for Halloween."

"You're a lifesaver. Put it all on the counter. Have you eaten?"

"Yeah, but I could do with another cup of coffee."

"Me, too. Excuse the unmade bed. I'm a little slow this morning."

"Does your finger hurt?"

"Compared to the rest of me it feels pretty good. I'm awful sore."

"Between climbing up and down that ladder and all that sawing and hammering yesterday, you got quite a workout." His knowing gaze darted over her baggy sweats. "Are you going to call in sick?"

"For a few aches and pains? I'd never do that." Wincing, she shuffled toward the coffee pot.

"I know a thing or two about knotted muscles," Hank said. "How about a massage?"

"You mean it?"

"Wouldn't have offered otherwise. Move that laptop off the bed and lie down on your stomach."

"Sometimes waiting to make the bed is a good thing," Deanna remarked as she complied.

Hank sat down beside her and raised her sweatshirt up her back. "I can't do as thorough a job with this in the way."

If he meant to seduce her he was in for disappointment. She was too darned sore. She glanced over her shoulder at him but didn't detect anything other than a genuine interest in making her feel better.

"Go ahead and take it off," she said, arching up and carefully stretching her arms over her head.

"You're wearing a different bra today. This one fastens in back. Okay to undo it?"

"Sure. Maybe I should take it off as well."

"That'll help."

As soon as she pulled the bra out from under her, Hank set to work kneading her back and shoulders. Moments later he paused. "Too hard?"

"A little, but I need this. Don't stop."

"Okay. If you change your mind, let me know."

Deanna added "magic hands" to Hank's long list of talents. After a time her muscles began to unclench. "You sure know your way around a massage," she purred.

"Most of the knots are gone. Time to work on your legs. Lift up for me and I'll get rid of those pants."

By his raspy voice he was aroused. Now that Deanna felt better, so was she was halfway there herself. She raised her hips, he gave a tug, and the sweat bottoms disappeared.

"'Juicy,' huh?"

She heard the smile in his tone and knew he was looking at the word scrawled across her behind. "It's the brand name," she explained.

"I like."

He started with her feet. "You painted your toenails."

Because she'd wanted to polish them before he saw her barefoot again. She forgot all about that as he proceeded upward to her calves and the backs of her thighs, turning her muscles to putty.

"I'll bet your glutes hurt, too." The rasp in his voice had deepened.

"Mm-hm."

He didn't ask her to remove her panties. His big, warm hands kneaded her behind—both heaven and torture. A different kind of ache flooded her body, making the crotch of her panties wet.

Avid, open-mouth kisses all over her back—an erogenous zone she'd never realized existed.

Wanting his mouth and hands all over her female parts and needing to see him, she turned onto her back.

Hank pulled off his own shirt and studied her with open longing. She scooted over a bit to make room for him.

After joining her on the bed he took her mouth, kissing her until the world narrowed to his taste and smell. Slowly and thoroughly he made his way down her body, toward the place that most needed his attention.

Her panties disappeared. He kissed her inner thighs, close, but not quite close enough. Filled with unbearable longing, she shifted restlessly. "Please, Hank."

He lifted her knees and put them over his shoulders. "How do those thigh muscles feel?"

"What muscles?"

He laughed softly, then got serious. Deanna grasped hold of his ears, urging him on. The delicious tension inside climbed to a fever pitch, then broke free. She squeezed his shoulders with her thighs and shattered.

When she flopped back to earth he was grinning.

"Proud of yourself, are you?" she teased.

"First time I've ever been caught in an ear grip and a thigh headlock."

"Sorry about that. I hope I didn't hurt you."

"You did—in the best way possible."

"Let me make you feel better." She reached for his strained zipper.

"Count on that, but not now." He checked his watch. "You need to get ready for work and meet your window and insulation people, and I need to order the drywall."

She'd nearly forgotten. Clutching the sheet, she sat up. "You never got your coffee."

"This was way more fun."

He left her satisfied and relaxed, again without asking for anything in return. He seemed in no hurry to have sex, which was reassuring. It was obvious he liked her for more than her body.

Deanna began to question her decision to slow down. Hank cared for her, so what was the point of waiting? On the other hand, why rush things?

Clearly she had some thinking to do.

22

"**H**appy Halloween!" Vi called out when Deanna entered the all but deserted building of the Guff's Lake Visitors and Convention Bureau on Thursday morning. "What do you think of my Minnie Mouse outfit?"

"It's cute."

"So are your new hat and gloves. Where's your costume?"

"I'll put it on when I get to the hotel. What pretty flowers."

Vi nodded. "Rick gave them to me—just because."

Deanna felt a pang of envy. No man had ever given her flowers.

"How about some candy?" Vi indicated a plastic pumpkin brimming with mini chocolates and other treats.

"No, thanks. I'm sure we'll have plenty at work." She smiled at Vi's fifty-something co-worker, Angie. "I like the purple witch hat and wig."

"I wear the same thing every year," Angie said. "I heard about your house. I'm so sorry."

"You know me—I've already put it behind me and

moved on." Which was mostly true. The solid progress at Oliver's and Deanna's budding relationship with Hank had lessened the sting of her loss. "By the way, I'm planning to sell the lot where the bungalow stood," she announced. She had the name of a real estate agent to market and sell it. "Tell everyone you know."

"We will." Vi eyed Deanna. "I know you didn't come all the way downtown just to see Angie and me in our Halloween outfits and tell us about the lot."

"I have extra time this morning, and we haven't seen each other or talked in way too long," Deanna said.

Not since before she'd helped Hank with the wiring. She needed to catch her friend up with a face-to-face and get Vi's take on things—without Angie eavesdropping. "Would you mind if I borrowed Vi for a coffee break?" she asked.

Vi was already reaching into the bottom drawer of her desk for her purse. "I'm ready for a break. I've been meaning to try Rocket Coffee, a new drive-thru that opened in the parking lot of the gas station a few blocks away. Shall I bring you back something, Angie?"

"No, thanks. Between my morning coffee and the chocolate, I've had enough caffeine for one day. You two have fun."

"I'll drive," Deanna offered as they exited into the morning sun. In the car, she pulled off the gloves and hat and handed them to Vi.

Her friend eyed them. "I'm dying to know what's going on with Hank, but first, tell me where you got this adorable set."

"He gave them to me."

"No kidding. When did that happen?"

"Tuesday, but let me backtrack to Monday." Deanna launched into the story. She was getting to the part about dinner at Hank's and his house tour when Vi interrupted.

"Turn here."

Deanna turned into the gas station and drove straight through to Rocket Coffee on the far side. Conversation stopped until two coffees sat snug in the car's cup holders and Deanna pulled away.

"Too bad I haven't finished my story," Deanna said as she pulled away from the drive-thru. "It'd be nice to sit down somewhere, sip our coffees, and talk."

"There's plenty of room to park around the corner of the building. We can stay in the car. You were at the part where you and Hank were about to have dinner at his place." Vi was all ears.

"You're really into this," Deanna teased as she parked.

"Hey, you're my BFF and this is the first time in ages you've spent a chunk of time with a man. Not just any man—Hank Gardener." Vi let out a dreamy sigh. "He bought you a hat and matching gloves and invited you to his house! Don't leave me dangling. I need details."

Deanna laughed. "Patience, Vi, I'm still on Monday. We picked up a pizza at Harvey's. After we ate Hank shared his Oreo cookie stash with me. Guess what? He also likes to dunk them in milk—in a bowl instead of a glass. Cool idea, huh?"

"I'll have to try that. The man shared his Oreos with you." Vi grinned. "Now you're talkin'. Go on."

"After dinner he offered to show me the house. He's made a ton of renovations."

"Did you see his bedroom?"

The room that had set the stage for everything that had happened since. "Yes, and it's huge. He took an old rambler with cramped rooms and transformed it into a beautiful, modern home."

"You had me at 'renovate.' I'm picturing him in a tool belt and no shirt. His pecs, those shoulders..." Vi fanned herself.

"I haven't seen him in a tool belt, but he does have a nice chest and abs."

"You've seen him shirtless? OMG, you and Hank are getting physical." Vi sat back. "Are you having sex?"

"Geez, Vi, some things are private. But no, not yet."

"Soon, though, right?"

"I'm trying to tell you about Monday night. The wiring thing went so well. Dinner, too. We were comfortable with each other, like friends relaxing together after a long day, and I didn't plan to kiss him let alone anything else. I'm pretty sure he felt the same way. It just happened."

And had continued Wednesday and Thursday mornings. They'd skipped today—Hank had needed to pick up the drywall he'd ordered and she'd wanted to talk with Vi.

He seemed to enjoy pleasuring Deanna without getting anything for himself. He didn't pressure her, either, while he waited for her to decide when to make love. A first in her life.

He made her feel special. His warmth and tenderness, the way he teased her and laughed at her jokes. His passion and how he touched her.

Was it any wonder she'd gone a little crazy? "There's something about him I can't resist," she summarized.

"Totally understandable." Val used her hands to mimic a balance scale. "Eight-date rule. Hank." She raised the hand representing Hank. "No contest—the sexy firefighter wins."

"Hank reminded me of the rule after we'd kissed for a while Monday night," Deana said.

"He brought that up? Most guys would let it go in hopes of getting lucky."

Another reason Deanna liked him so much. For reminding her when sexual desire blurred her own boundaries. "Hank isn't most guys. He didn't want me regretting anything later. And FYI, the eight-date rule is alive and well. As I explained to him, we spent hours talking in the hotel bar one night. We worked together the whole day Monday, then shared dinner. All that time with each other equals at least eight dates."

"Makes sense to me."

"Anyway, I learned so much Monday that I asked if I could help him replace siding on Tuesday."

"And he said yes?"

Deanna nodded. "I didn't have gloves and we were going to be outdoors all day, so he stopped at the drugstore and bought me a pair of work gloves. They were also hosting a fundraiser for a women's shelter inside. That's where he picked up the hat and glove set."

"What a guy."

"I know. At first I was wary of him. But everything he does and says proves that for once, my judgment and my heart are in total sync."

Vi beamed. "Do you realize how long it's been since you've talked about a guy like this? We should double date sometime."

"That'd be fun."

Vi checked her watch. "It's time for Angie's break. I'd better get back."

"And I need to get to work early so that I can change into my costume." Deanna started the car.

"You never said what your costume is this year."

"I'm going to be a firefighter. Hank loaned me an old shirt and hat."

"That I have to see. Send me a photo."

"Will do."

"I'm sure he'd like to see you all dressed up. Are you going to his place after work?"

They hadn't discussed it. "I don't know," Deanna said. "You know how it goes at the Hearthstone. Halloween night will either be super busy or very slow. Hank gets up early. By the time I get home he could already be asleep."

"You're just across the yard from him. Run over there and check. It's a shame you work opposite schedules. Have you talked about what will happen after you move?"

One week from tomorrow. Deanna shook her head. "Not yet."

Lately she and Hank had been too busy in bed to talk much about anything. After a mere two days she'd come to anticipate the intense pleasure he gave her in the morning and couldn't imagine not enjoying a passionate hour together. She'd certainly missed him today. "I'm sure we'll make time to see each other," she added.

But she couldn't help wondering about the future. They needed to talk about that and about what they expected from each other—provided they were an actual couple.

Were they? Did Hank even want a relationship?

Of course he did. Otherwise he wouldn't treat her as if she mattered so much. He'd take what he wanted instead of waiting.

Despite her self-assurances the doubts persisted. "How can I be sure he wants me for myself and not my body?" she asked.

"You know how it is with guys—they can't separate one from the other."

She had a point. Deanna bit her lip.

"You're having second thoughts." Vi frowned. "I don't understand. You just told me that your heart and judgment are finally in sync."

"I guess I'm still a little insecure. I tell myself to move slowly but when I'm with him slow is the last thing I want."

"Is he pressuring you?"

"Not at all. He even tried to warn me away. He's been so thoughtful and good to me, better than any man I've ever known." Deanna hesitated.

"But?"

"For me, sex changes everything. I want it, but I'm scared."

"You're falling for him."

Deanna let out a huge sigh. "I already have."

"Does he know this?"

"He hasn't a clue and for now, that's how I want to keep it."

"Tell him you're not ready for sex. If he really cares for you he'll keep waiting. Although now that things between you are hot and heavy you may not be able to stop."

A definite problem. For all her fears, Deanna spent a huge amount of time fantasizing about completing the act of love with Hank. To the point that she sometimes thought she'd go mad if they didn't make love soon.

Twitchy and restless, she shifted in her seat. "I'm so

confused. I don't want to stop, even though I know I should."

"Remember when I saw a therapist last year?" Vi said. "Let me try one of her tricks on you. Don't stop and think, just blurt your answer to this question. If you could have anything you wanted out of life, what would you choose?"

"To be with Hank."

The instant Deanna uttered the words the uncertainty faded away and everything clicked into place.

Vi nodded. "There you go."

By the time Deanna pulled over to let Vi out she'd made up her mind. She wanted Hank—all of him. "Talking about this helped a lot," she said.

"That's what best friends are for. What are you going to do?"

"Make love with him."

"That's what I'd do. Smooches."

They exchanged hugs and Vi slipped out of the car.

On the way to work Deanna mulled over her decision and how to tell Hank.

Maybe she'd show him instead. The next time they were alone together there would be no holding back. She'd make sure of that.

HANGING drywall was tedious and slow going, and doing it alone didn't help. Hank looked forward to working with Max, Nate, and Tony tomorrow. Things would be a lot more interesting and move along faster. With their help, they'd no doubt finish the job tomorrow.

The window installers showed up early in the afternoon. Hank stuck around until they left, then headed to the drugstore to pick up Halloween candy for the evening ahead. He bought a ton of the stuff to feed the hordes of trick-or-treaters sure to knock on his door from around dusk until who knew when.

Deanna was likely to be just as busy at the Hearthstone and would probably get home late. He might not see her tonight and regretted that.

He'd missed fooling around in her bed this morning, making her thrash and moan until she climaxed. He got hard thinking about it.

Yeah, he was playing with fire and would suffer for it later, but stopping what they'd started was not an option.

They were great together and all he wanted was to be with her, gloved deep in her moist heat until they both lost their minds.

It couldn't happen soon enough.

By nine-thirty the parade of trick-or-treaters had slowed to a trickle. And a good thing, as only one pack of gum and a Tootsie Pop remained in the candy bowl. Hank was about to cut the lights and call it a night when the doorbell rang.

Deanna stood in the yellow glow of his front-porch light, with her parka zipped up tight and the firefighter's hat he'd loaned her on her head. It was several sizes too big and tilted slightly to one side. She looked cute and sexy. He couldn't wait to see what his shirt looked like on her.

"Trick or treat," she said with a bright grin.

"I like you in my hat." He gestured her inside and closed the door. "How was work?"

"We were slammed tonight." She took off the hat and followed him to the kitchen. "This morning I had coffee with my friend, Vi. She dressed as Minnie Mouse."

"Fun. How did she like your costume?"

"I didn't put it on until I got to work, but she loved the photos I sent. You should have seen the flowers she got from her boyfriend."

"For Halloween?"

Deanna shook her head. "Just because."

"Nice guy." Was there a reason she'd mentioned this? While Hank mentally scratched his head, she answered his unspoken question.

"Hey, I don't expect flowers from you. I just thought it was cool."

He relaxed. "Why don't you take your coat off?"

"Not yet. I heard from the window company that the windows are in."

"They look good."

"That's a relief. How's the drywall installation going?"

"I got a fair amount done. With Max, Tony, and Nate pitching in tomorrow, we should be able to finish up by the end of the day."

"Wonderful. You and your friends are such great guys."

Her eyes beamed with the admiration and respect Hank had come to anticipate almost as much as her passion.

Esteem he didn't deserve.

What kind of jerk hides his sins from the woman he cares for?

"What do you recommend as a thank-you?" she asked.

"Beer and dinner."

"That's easy. Since I'll be working tomorrow night, I'll give you money to take them out."

"All right."

She frowned at the candy bowl. "There's hardly anything left in here."

"I'm down to the dregs but I could rustle up some Oreos and milk."

"I have something even better in mind."

She touched her tongue to her upper lip and gave him a sultry look that obliterated everything but his desire. He reached for her.

23

A s ready as Deanna was to be with Hank she'd never done anything quite this bold. That explained why she was trembling inside.

He started to unzip her parka but she shook her finger. "Easy there, big guy." Fighting her sudden case of nerves, she pulled a chair out from the table and pushed him into it. "Sit."

His eyes narrowed a fraction. "What for?"

"Just do it."

As soon as he complied she stepped out of reach, grasped the zipper on her parka and tugged it down. Slowly, seductively, stopping just above breast level.

"What happened to the shirt I lent you— Wait, are you naked on top?"

"Watch and see."

Hank sat back with a smoldering look that incinerated any anxiety.

As she drew the zipper down the rest of the way he swallowed audibly.

"Get over here stat, woman."

"Yes, sir."

Her parka disappeared and so did his pullover sweater. He hauled her onto his lap. Bare skin. Eager, consuming kisses. Mounting passion that made her wet.

Suddenly Hank broke away. Breathing hard he grasped her chin. "I'm about five seconds from the point of no return. Are you ready for that?"

"I come to you topless on a freezing night and you have to ask?"

He shook his head and grinned.

"You're pleased."

"Honey, you have no idea."

He ran his thumbnail lightly across her nipple. Deanna sucked in a breath. "Tell me you have condoms."

"As a matter of fact, I bought a jumbo box at the drugstore this afternoon."

After that there were no more words. Until without warning, he wrenched his mouth from hers. "I want you in my bed. Under me. Now."

Cupping her rear end in his capable hands he rose, lifting her as if she weighed no more than a bag of chips. Deanna wrapped her thighs around his hips and clung to him.

She scarcely registered his heart thundering against hers before he caught her in a searing kiss.

Somehow they made it to the bedroom. Hank flipped a switch and the bedside lamp flared to life.

He set her on her feet to fold the bedding back, then pulled her into another kiss she felt in all her aching parts.

Locking eyes, they shed their remaining clothes.

For all the times he'd seen her completely naked this was her first look at him. He was lean and muscled and gloriously aroused—huge.

And all hers.

"You're grinning again," she said.

"Because you like what you see."

"Just how would you know that?"

"Your face is an open book."

"And here I thought I was good at hiding my feelings."

"Nope, and that's beautiful. Don't ever change, Deanna."

Filled with love she opened her arms. "Make love with me, Hank."

He tumbled her so fast onto the bed she didn't have time to blink. Yet for all his eagerness he took his time, teasing his way down her body until she was ready to go up in flames.

This time she wanted to give before she took. As he reached her most needy place she batted him away. "I'm in charge tonight and it's my turn. On your back."

"Uh, yes sir, ma'am."

She knelt over him and lightly flicked his nipples. He shuddered and his erection jerked. Smiling to herself she nuzzled his chest, his belly, taking her sweet time just as he did with her.

"Deanna," he moaned and raised up.

"Down, you." Hand on his chest, she pushed him flat on the mattress.

He could have overpowered her in a heartbeat. Instead, he let her have her way.

"This is torture," he ground out as she blew air on his arousal.

"It's called payback. Just wait." She licked his length, then took him in her mouth.

"Stop." He gripped her head in his hands.

"Why?" she asked, widening her eyes.

"You know why—when I come it will be inside you."

"What are we waiting for? Open that box of condoms."

Hank sheathed himself and turned back to her.

She'd never had sex with the lights on. "Shouldn't we turn off the lamp?"

He shook his head. "When I'm buried in you and you scream my name I want to see you."

How could she turn him down? "All right."

Supporting his weight on his arms he covered her. She waited for him to enter her, but he held himself still.

"Why are you holding back?" she pleaded in frustration.

His jaws clenched. " I don't want to rush our first time. I'm trying to maintain some control here."

"Forget control and hurry up."

"You're the boss." One thrust and he filled her. "Good?" he asked.

She could barely speak for the exquisite sensation. She closed her eyes. "Really good."

"Look at me, Deanna."

The instant she met his gaze he began to move. Heaven.

Delicious tension spiraled between her legs. Tighter and tighter until it burst in a convulsion of pleasure that went on and on. Deanna cried out and Hank gave a savage growl.

Release. Completion.

When the world righted itself some time later he was still deep inside her.

Kissing her gently, he rolled to a sitting position. "I'll be right back with a washcloth."

He padded to the bathroom.

Basking in the afterglow Deanna heaved a contented sigh. And knew there was no going back. From now on she belonged to Hank. Body, heart, and soul.

She prayed he didn't hurt her.

SEX HAD NEVER BEEN like this. Staggered by the deep connection he'd forged with Deanna in bed tonight, Hank braced himself against the bathroom sink.

Had to be the eye contact. He'd never locked into a woman's gaze while they both climaxed, wasn't sure why he'd wanted to. Exposing himself to Deanna like that had been the most intimate act of his life.

Powerful. Mind-blowing.

Confusing.

He didn't understand the emotions crowding his chest, but they scared him. On the heels of that, his conscience, drowned out by his all-consuming hunger for her, kicked into full gear.

Hunger for her body and for the awesome respect and admiration that warmed the dark recesses of his soul. He needed her, needed that, the same way he needed air.

Too bad he wasn't half the man she thought he was.

He scrubbed his hand over his face. What the hell was he going to do now?

Tell her what you did.

Little late for that.

Ready to suggest she go home so they could both get some much-needed rest, he wet a washcloth with warm water and returned to the bedroom.

In the threshold he paused. The lamp's warm halo of light spilled over her motionless form. Already asleep. The rosy flush of desire still colored her skin and her hair spread across his empty pillow.

So beautiful, he ached. He padded softly toward her.

Her eyelids fluttered open. "Hi," she murmured with a radiant smile that lit him up inside.

His mouth went dry. "Hey, sleepyhead." Awash in tenderness he gave her the washcloth. "For you. Drop it on the floor when you're done."

Then because he couldn't ask her to leave he lay down beside her and flipped off the light.

She burrowed close and fell back into her peaceful slumber. While Hank lay in pain and torment. For being a sorry excuse of a man. For liking her too damn much. And for screwing things up worse than he already had.

He blew out a heavy breath.

"Are you all right?" she asked, sounding drowsy.

No. He needed her out of here so he could think straight. "It's late and we both have busy days tomorrow. I think we should—"

"Make love?"

She slid her hand down his belly, straight to his cock. White-hot lust took over and all coherent thought faded from his mind.

24

Deanna awoke alone in Hank's big bed. Squinting through the dark she glanced at the clock. Five a.m.

Down the hall the kitchen door clicked shut. He must be going out for his morning run—despite having only a few hours' sleep. How did he have the energy?

Although she felt pretty darned good herself. Make that wonderful. Smiling and stretching, she considered dozing until he returned. Then ditched the idea. She didn't want to overstay her welcome.

Humming, she dressed, which thanks to showing up topless last night didn't take long. And hadn't that worked out well. Hank had loved her mini striptease. Loved her with a thoroughness that still resonated through her body.

And yet...

Not long after their second lovemaking he'd turned away and slept facing the wall. Maybe he didn't enjoy cuddling all night. Or... What?

Deanna racked her brain. When he'd returned from the bathroom after their first time he'd started to say something. He may have wanted her to go home.

If only she'd let him finish his thought instead of initiating more sex.

Not that he'd seemed to mind. The second time had been amazing. Yet thinking back, she realized something had changed. Because the light had been off and she couldn't see his face? No, he felt different, as if he were holding back.

Uneasy, she made the bed, then headed for the kitchen to get her parka and leave. A note lay propped against the toaster.

Gone running before I meet the guys at the B&B. I'll treat them to dinner tonight. Coffeemaker ready to go. Help yourself to anything from the fridge. Talk later.

A perfectly reasonable, yet disappointing note. He couldn't ask her to stick around for when he returned or mention wanting to see her again soon?

Drowning in need and pleasure last night, she'd been too distracted to broach the subject of the future. Hank hadn't brought it up, either. Deanna had no idea where their relationship stood.

She'd assumed they'd shared something meaningful and special, but for all she knew Hank showered every woman he took to bed with the same attention and focus.

There was no need to jump to hasty conclusions, she told herself as she attempted to reason away the hollow feeling in her heart. Hank cared a lot. Everything he'd said and done the past few weeks and especially last night proved it.

Still, she couldn't shake the feeling that something was off, and that maybe she'd moved too fast, after all.

~

A HARD RUN to and around Guff's Lake failed to lift Hank's dismal spirits. Ditto on the bracing shower and double shot of caffeine he'd picked up at the Coffee Shack, which wasn't far from Deanna's property.

Blame it on last night. Letting Deanna stay over, making love with her twice when he should have sent her home...

What a piece of work he was.

Before heading to Oliver's he bought a dozen doughnuts. He arrived at the B&B seconds ahead of Max, Nate, Tony, and his boxer, Boomer. They pulled up behind him and exited Nate's Expedition.

"You look like hell," Max greeted him. "Bad night?"

Nate snickered. "Judging by the love bite on his neck, I'd say our buddy is suffering from a serious lack of sleep. If I had that 'problem,' I'd be smiling from ear to ear."

Not if he'd effed up big time, as Hank had. He snatched the doughnuts from the passenger seat.

Woofing, Boomer strained at his leash to get at the sugary treats. Tony restrained him. "None for you, boy, but I'm ready for mine."

As soon as Hank opened the box, he passed it around.

"Are those plat stakes in the ground near where the bungalow stood?" Max asked while he chomped on his maple bar.

Hank nodded. "Deanna plans to sell that part of her property. Spread the word."

"Will do."

Nate blew on his hands. "We going inside or what? It's frickin' cold out."

After unlocking the door to the B&B, Hank and his buds tromped inside.

"Nice and warm in here," Nate said, nodding at the

new insulation visible behind the bare studs. "New windows, too."

"Just in time for winter," Tony commented. "It's been colder and wetter than usual for weeks. Patching the siding the other day must've been a real bitch."

"You forget Hank had Deanna with him," Max pointed out.

Three knowing grins followed.

"Gotta hand it to you, man." Nate saluted him. "Getting her to keep you warm—smooth move."

He didn't know the half of it. "I didn't 'get her' to do anything," Hank clarified. "She asked to help."

Nate nodded. "Everyone at the station has been talking about how she wants to learn all about renovation. She's cool."

"You mean hot," Tony corrected.

"That's enough." Hank's glare included them all. "Yesterday I finished a couple rooms upstairs but there's plenty left to do up there. Max, you and I will work up there. When we finish we'll come down and help Nate and Tony with the main floor. If all goes well we'll finish in time to grab beer and pizza courtesy of Deanna. Have at it."

"You're involved with her," Max commented while he and Hank measured boards for the walls.

No point denying it. "I didn't plan to be, but yeah."

"Makes sense to me—she's good people. You must have finally accepted that what happened to her bungalow isn't on you. It's about damn time."

If only. A man didn't move past something like that. Hell, Hank felt worse by the day. He got real busy cutting drywall.

Max raised his eyebrows. "You haven't. Does Deanna know you blame yourself?"

"Nope." Lips compressed and eyes narrowed, Hank warned his bud off.

No such luck. Max crossed his arms. "You need to make peace with yourself, man. If that means telling her you hold yourself responsible for the loss of her house, then do it."

Like Hank wasn't aware of that. He snarled a string of expletives. "You through?"

Unfazed, Max shrugged. "For now."

Grunting, Hank hefted a board and set it in place. Hard physical labor temporarily banished his self-loathing from his conscious mind, but the whole ugly dilemma festered inside him.

He was so damn sick of not being able to look at himself in the mirror without disgust.

By the time everyone congratulated themselves on finishing the job late in the afternoon, he silently acknowledged that he couldn't live with himself any longer until he made things right.

It was time to man up and admit his failings to Deanna.

In no mood to linger after dinner, he pleaded fatigue and headed home to wait for her.

She wouldn't finish work for several more hours and would likely be as tired as him, but he needed to talk to her tonight.

After that, he doubted she'd ever want to see him again.

25

D ue to an unusually slow night at the Hearthstone the manager sent Deanna home early. Not in the best mood due to lack of sleep and not one word from Hank all day, she didn't argue.

They'd both been busy and normally she wouldn't have given his silence a second thought. But with the uneasiness she'd felt this morning she'd have welcomed the reassurance. Instead, the sense that something was wrong had grown steadily until she wanted to howl.

Worrying wouldn't help. Besides, Hank was out with his crewmates, enjoying dinner and beer, and she didn't expect to see him tonight. She didn't want to sit at home and brood, either. She phoned Bea. "I got off early tonight and I'd love to see you. Why don't I stop by Chicken D'Lite and pick us up a couple of dinners?" That was the older woman's favorite takeout. "Unless you already ate."

"Not since lunch. It would be lovely to see you."

"I'll be there soon."

In no time Deanna was sitting at her friend's table enjoying the meal and catching up.

"I noticed that Hank and his friends spent the day at Oliver's," Bea said. "My, they're a handsome lot. What were they doing?"

"Installing drywall."

"Isn't it lucky your Hank is so skilled with his hands."

He certainly was. "He's not mine."

"You're mistaken, Deanna. When I brought over cake and coffee the day you two helped with the wiring, I saw how he looked at you."

Deanna wasn't blind—she'd noticed. But she'd been around that block too many times not to know that aside from sex, hot looks and sweet words didn't necessarily mean anything.

Not about to discuss sex with her elderly friend, she bit into her chicken.

"If you ever want to talk about him, I'm a good listener," Bea commented. "I won't blab and tell, like some people in town."

She meant Betty Randall, the biggest gossip in town.

"I totally trust you," Deanna assured her. "If I had anything important to say, believe me, I'd share it right now. The truth is, I don't know where things stand between Hank and me."

Clarity would be nice. She needed answers, sooner than later—no matter what the outcome.

Doubt and uncertainty ruined her appetite. Picking at the remains of her meal she changed the subject. "I contacted a real estate agent this morning. We're meeting later in the week. Cross your fingers the land sells fast."

Bea crossed the gnarled fingers of both hands.

"I haven't been inside Oliver's in days. I think I'll go

over after dinner and take a look around. Why don't you come with me?" Deanna asked.

Her friend's eyes lit up. "I'd like that."

As they strolled through the house a short while later, Deanna marveled at what Hank and his friends had accomplished.

"This place is coming along." Bea smiled and shook her head. "I can't believe how much work has been done since Hank came into your life. He's a keeper."

Deanna thought so, but that depended on Hank.

Oblivious, her friend rattled on. "Even though this place is unfinished it feels solid and snug."

Deanna agreed. "Even with the furnace turned down."

"What's next on the agenda?"

"Hiring someone to plaster the walls so that I can prime and paint them."

"At this rate you'll open for business in time for the Christmas season."

"I wish, but there's still a lot to do—finishing the kitchen, carpeting, designing a sign to hang out front, flyers and promotional pieces. And don't forget curtains and furniture. If the land sells right away, I'll be able to get most of it done in the near future. If not... Saving up will take awhile."

"No matter—as you always say, one step at a time. It's all so exciting." Bea's eyes sparkled. "Your dreams are finally coming true."

Her enthusiasm and support did wonders for Deanna's spirits. By the time they hugged each other good night, her optimism had been restored.

"Slow and steady," she reminded herself on the uneventful drive home. Success meant keeping her eyes on the goal and moving forward one step at a time.

Yet once again she'd failed to apply the same important principle to her love life. Her haste to be with Hank had suppressed the need for cautiousness.

It wasn't his fault. From the beginning she'd pushed the relationship. Making love last night, then staying over... She hoped she hadn't ruined everything.

Anxious all over again and unhappy with herself, she changed her mind. Instead of talking to Hank about their relationship, she'd pull back, give him space, and let him take the lead.

Best not to be awake when he came home. She'd climb into bed early and catch up on much-needed sleep.

Ready to do just that she pulled into the driveway. To her surprise, the CRV was in its usual spot, and Hank's house was ablaze with light. The evening with his friends had ended early.

Before she braked to a stop his kitchen door opened. He started toward her with a determined stride.

He'd been waiting for her. Her misgivings began to fade and she smiled—until she noted his grim expression. And knew she'd been right to worry.

He was going to end the relationship.

Deanna's heart stuttered in her chest. She longed to back out and drive away, but that was impossible. Never mind—she would face him clear-eyed and strong. He would not see her pain.

Squaring her shoulders, she exited the car.

26

R eady or not, Hank's own private D-Day had arrived.

As bad as he needed to clear his conscience, he dreaded the aftermath—to the point that he felt sick inside. But he couldn't put it off any longer. He greeted Deanna with a somber nod. "You're home early."

"Tonight was as slow as last night was busy."

Her raised head and cool eyes alerted him that she was pissed off. And he hadn't even mentioned the real story about the fire yet.

"I should have called today," he said.

"That's why you're so solemn." Her rigid spine relaxed and her chin lowered as if she was relieved. "Hey, you had a lot on your plate. I walked through Oliver's earlier with Bea and I saw all that you and your friends did. You're amazing."

She beamed the admiration and respect that made Hank feel ten feet tall. Not for much longer.

Something wrenched painfully in his chest. Unable to look her in the eye, he kicked at the blacktop. "Come in the house. We need to talk."

Her hands twisted together. "Okay."

In the kitchen, Hank grabbed a liter of pop and two glasses and set them on the table. He and Deanna sat down.

"Thirsty?" he asked.

"No, thanks."

Once he filled his glass there was nothing else to do but come clean. As scared as if he were facing a firing squad, his throat too constricted to swallow, he bypassed the pop. "When your bungalow burned down..." He had to stop and pull it together.

Deanna frowned. "Wait—I thought this conversation was about us."

"It is. I don't know how to put this except to say it straight. It's my fault your bungalow burned to the ground."

She shook her head. "That's not true. You and your crewmates did everything possible to save it."

"True, but the difference between me and them is, they did everything right. I fell short. If someone else had been assigned to the job I had that day, that house would still be standing."

The frown deepened. "You're not making any sense."

"Let me explain the workings of a fire. In a nutshell, a firefighter is trained to pay close attention to the flames. The smoke is equally important. Its color, intensity, and direction indicate what will happen next."

"I remember from when you took that refresher class. You said firefighters study smoke to figure out what their next move will be."

Should have figured she'd paid attention. He almost smiled. "That class happened because I requested it after my failure to read the smoke cost you your home."

There, it was out. Avoiding the condemnation sure to be all over her face, he slid his untouched glass around the table. "I should have told you right away."

"Why didn't you?"

The soft, non-accusatory tone compelled him to look at her. Her bewildered expression, void of anger, gave him hope.

But she'd asked a question he needed to answer.

He considered making up some flimsy reason for hiding the truth but he'd lied enough. "I didn't want you to lose respect for me."

For once, Deanna was impossible to read. Still and quiet, almost placid.

"You wouldn't accept money from the benefit fund," he went on. "I figured if I helped fix up your bed & breakfast I could keep your respect and make up for what I did at the same time."

She sat back. "You've been working on Oliver's to salve your conscience?"

"Something like that. But it didn't work."

He didn't understand the stark resignation in her eyes.

"I'll bet you offered me the use of your camper for the same reason."

He let his silence speak for him.

"And all this time I thought you cared about me. Instead, I'm just another charity case." She compressed her trembling lips.

"It wasn't like that, Deanna. Yes, I started off wanting to help you to atone for my sins, but I never considered you a charity case. You're too proud and independent for that. Almost right away my reason for helping you changed. I did it because I wanted to, because the better I knew you the more I cared. You mean an awful lot to me."

She didn't seem to hear, looked right past him, addressing the empty space over his shoulder as if she couldn't stand to look at him. "Everyone makes mistakes. God knows, I've made my share. I could have excused you for that. It's the lies I can't forgive."

No sign now of her previous calm. Anger simmered from every pore.

He deserved that and more. "I've always said I'm bad news. You should have listened."

"That doesn't justify what you did." She was shaking now. "I thought you were different from other men, but you're just like all the rest. You lie to get what you want and to hell with the consequences."

A third-degree burn would have wounded him less. He flinched but bore his just desserts. "I never meant to hurt you, Deanna. We started something good together. I don't want to lose you."

"It's a little too late for that."

She stumbled up and made for the door, slamming it behind her.

~

REFUSING to stay in the camper one more night, Deanna packed her belongings. She had a few more things than when she'd moved in, but not much.

Hot tears gathered behind her eyes, begging for release. She would not cry on Hank's property. Or waste one second feeling sorry for herself. She blinked them back.

Mad? You betcha. At herself for trusting Hank when she knew better than to fall for his sweet talk and tender looks. From the start she'd suspected he was too good to be real, but just like always she'd allowed her heart to overpower her common sense.

Believing his every word, letting his glances warm her clear to her toes, melting like wax against a flame —all of that was on her.

She seemed destined to repeat the same mistakes over and over. But this... This felt like hitting rock bottom, more jarring and painful than anything she'd ever experienced.

Guided by the camper's lone porch light, possessions in her arms, she made her way across the grass, to the driveway and her car. She deposited everything in the open hatchback, then returned to the camper for a second load. Except for the clothing in the closet, that was it.

In the camper again and fueled by anger, she scrubbed every surface clean until she'd erased all traces of herself.

When she finished, the place looked just as it had the day Hank had first shown it to her. Clean and devoid of any personal effects—as if she'd never been here at all. The anger drained away, leaving her sad and empty.

It was almost midnight when she pulled the last of her clothing, mostly work pants and blouses still on the hangers, from the closet. Purse swinging from her shoulder, she picked her way across the yard.

If she was smart, she'd give up men for good. No— she needed sex. All right then, she'd give up love, maybe take—

Looking inward instead of where she was going, Deanna caught the toe of her shoe where the yard met the blacktop. She stumbled and fell, scattering hangers, clothing, and the contents of her purse across the driveway.

Despite catching herself with her hands out she whacked her chin hard. "Ow!"

She struggled to a sitting position. Her chin and one knee hurt, and both palms burned. She'd really scraped herself up.

This time when her eyes filled she couldn't stop the tears. Scooting across the cold, unyielding blacktop she collected the contents of her purse. Including a pack of tissues she put to immediate use.

Wouldn't you know the light in Hank's kitchen flicked on and his door opened.

"Deanna? Are you all right?" He started toward her.

Crap. She refused to let him see her cry. Pride firmly intact, she dabbed her eyes, blew her nose, and pushed to her feet. "I tripped, but I'm okay."

He reached her. "It's late. What are you doing out here?"

"What does it look like? I'm leaving." She placed her purse on the hood of the car, then bent down to scoop up clothing, hoping she didn't smear blood on anything.

"Let me do that." Gently pushing her aside, Hank gathered the items.

"I don't want your help." She tried to elbow him aside, but the big ox refused to budge.

"You're bleeding." After he laid her clothing in the back seat, he tipped her chin toward the motion detector lights to get a better look. "That's a nasty scrape. Come inside and I'll fix you up."

He was a trained paramedic so she didn't argue. She limped into the kitchen behind him.

The open pop bottle, Hank's still-full glass, the chair she'd pushed from the table—since she'd left nothing had been touched. That wasn't like him.

He sat her on a chair, then left to get what he needed. He returned and with infinite gentleness cleaned her chin and palms. He bandaged her hands, rolled up both legs of her jeans, and took care of her bloodied knee before carefully rolling her pant legs back down.

She wanted to melt. Damn him for his tenderness.

"All done." He set a tube of antibacterial cream in front of her. "Apply this to the abrasions once or twice a day."

Deanna considered rejecting the ointment but she needed it. Besides, she was too spent and defeated to argue. "I have something for you, too, but it's in my purse, which I left outside."

She made a move to rise but Hank's hand on her shoulder stayed her. "You sit. I'll get it."

As soon as he placed her purse on the table she dug out her checkbook and wrote him a check. "This is for the rent I still owe and partial payment for the work you did for me. I'll pay the rest as soon as I can."

The amount of the check put her right back to square one, with as little money as she'd had the day after the fire. Never mind—the busy winter tourist season was just around the corner. With the tips she was sure to earn she'd settle her debt to Hank in no time. Then like always, she'd move on without his or anyone's help.

He started to say something, then stopped himself. Smart man.

"I cleaned the Scamp. This is yours." She laid the key to the camper on top of the check. "Please give me the key to Oliver's."

He blew out a breath and handed it to her. "It's late. At least stay until morning."

That she was exhausted enough to consider the idea made her want to weep, although she couldn't have explained why. But no, pride and what little dignity she had left wouldn't allow that. "I can't, Hank."

"Where will you stay?"

Not at Oliver's. She didn't have a sleeping bag. Besides, the thought of Bea seeing her car there in the morning and asking questions... Deanna shuddered. "The hotel—where else?"

"Can we talk about this?"

Fresh tears lurked dangerously close to the surface. Somehow she held them back. She shook her head and stood. Slung her purse on her shoulder and walked through the door.

She got into her car and managed to drive a few blocks down the road before she pulled over and fell apart.

27

"These goat cheese appetizers are out of this world," Vi said and reached for another.

Deanna had met her friend at Barclay's, a restaurant on the north side of town, for dinner. Tuesday was ladies' night with drinks half-price.

Vi nudged the appetizer plate Deanna's way. "Try one."

"Nice," Deanna said when she finished hers.

"You said the same thing about your cocktail. Is this a funeral or a party? I know it's only been two weeks since you and Hank broke up, but we're supposed to be having fun."

"You're right." Deanna pasted a smile on her face. "You haven't mentioned last weekend." Vi had taken Rick to a cousin's wedding in Medford, where he'd met the entire family. "Did Rick survive?"

"Like a champ. Everyone adored him. He even charmed Uncle Buck, and you know what a grump he is. Rick liked them, too, and is actually looking forward to Thanksgiving. That's only two weeks from now—can you believe it? In my head it should still be August."

Which seemed a lifetime ago. Back then, blissfully

unaware of what was to come, Deanna had been working and dreaming and planning and minding her own business. Her heart had been intact and so had the bungalow.

She was over the whole bungalow thing and was trying hard to heal her heart. Which unfortunately was taking a lot longer than falling in love had.

"Rick really loves you," she said.

"And I'm crazy about him." Vi's smile was pure joy. "He's my Mr. Right."

Envious but happy for her friend, Deanna sighed. "Lucky you."

"Don't I know it. What are you doing for Thanksgiving? Are you planning to see your parents?"

Deanna shook her head. "My dad will probably spend part of the day with his mistress and Mom will get all upset. I can't handle that." Lately, she had enough trouble holding herself together. "Besides, they'll be here for a few days over Christmas. I'll be spending Thanksgiving with Bea. We're going to roast a turkey with all the trimmings."

The chitchat continued through the meal. Deanna thought she was doing her part to keep the conversation lively when Vi put a halt to the charade.

"I'm not having much fun, and neither are you. We both have to work tomorrow—we may as well go home."

Unable to argue with that, Deanna signaled the waiter for the check.

"Maybe you should cut Hank some slack," Vi said as they dug out their wallets.

"Are you serious? From day one, he lied to me. There's no way to get past that."

"Only because you refuse to do it."

Deanna's jaw dropped. "Who are you and what

have you done with my sympathetic and supportive BFF?"

"I mean it, Dee. You said he's called you four or five times. If it were me, I'd call him back."

"You'd forgive a man who lied to you?" Deanna clucked her tongue in disbelief.

"We're not talking about me. Remember why Hank did it—he didn't want you to lose respect for him. He never cheated on you and he did finally tell you the truth."

"Not until after we had sex and I'd fallen for him hook, line, and sinker."

"As I recall, you were in love with him before you had sex. He didn't force you to do either one."

"That's beside the point." Deanna narrowed her eyes. "Why are you defending him?"

"Because I've never seen you this miserable."

Vi was so right. A broken heart had never hurt this bad. But then, Deanna had never loved a man as deeply and completely as she did Hank.

"From everything you've said, Hank is a great guy," Vi continued. "Heck, he could be your Mr. Right. Yes, he slipped up, but like the rest of us, he's human."

"I don't lie, Vi. Neither do you."

"All I'm suggesting is, don't write him off so fast."

"I already have. Quit worrying about me. I'm the queen of bouncing back from whatever misfortune life throws my way, remember? I'll get over him and move on."

Eventually.

~

EVERYONE at the station had heard about Hank's split

with Deanna. He didn't want to talk about it and to his relief, they all left him alone.

Unlike Carolyn Block. Two days after Deanna had left for good, his neighbor had been all up in his business, wanting to know where she was.

"She moved," Hank had replied.

Carolyn had given him a dirty look. "She wasn't supposed to leave for another week. Otto and I really liked her."

Since then, every time he saw the woman her eyes shot daggers at him. As if he didn't feel lousy enough.

Monday was the first day of his month-long paramedic rotation, which he shared with Adam and Ethan. As always the team fielded plenty of calls, providing a welcome break from his gloomy thoughts.

Tuesday was particularly hectic. On the drive to the station after racing an eighty-year-old man in cardiac arrest to the ER, Adam glanced over his shoulder at Hank. "Good work, buddy. You saved that guy's life."

"As would you if you'd performed the CPR," Hank said. "We're a team—we saved him."

And that felt good. His personal life sucked, but work kept him sane and gave him a reason to get up in the morning.

At the wheel, Ethan shook his head. "Three emergencies since lunch. I'm ready for a break."

While Ethan and Adam rehashed the afternoon's calls so far, Hank tuned out. He didn't feel much like talking. Damn, he missed Deanna. He'd finally met the perfect woman and he'd blown it.

Figured.

"How about you, Hank?" Adam asked.

"Uh, could you repeat that?"

"Not important. This thing with Deanna has done a real number on you, and that concerns me."

As second in command to the captain, Adam and his opinion mattered. Well aware of the black cloud that had descended on him, Hank couldn't argue the point. But Adam had put him on the line and he felt defensive. He stiffened. "I haven't let that interfere with the job, have I?"

"No, but it'd be good to see you in a better place. You like her, huh?"

"A lot." More than any woman he'd been with.

"How long since you split up?"

"Three weeks and change." Long, bleak days that seemed to have no end in sight.

"As a guy who's been there, I feel ya. You should talk to her."

"I called her a bunch of times," Hank admitted. "She didn't pick up and never phoned me back. She doesn't want to hear from me." He muttered to himself, "Hell, I wouldn't, either."

"There's your problem," Adam said. "If you see yourself as a jerk, why should she believe otherwise?"

Ethan glanced at Hank in the rearview mirror. "You're not perfect, but you're no jerk. Do you think I'd trust you with my life if you were? Forget the phone and think outside the box. Some of the ladies I've known have found extremely creative ways to get my attention that sure worked on me." He grinned.

As a part-time sax player in a jazz band, Ethan drew interest from more women than any guy deserved. Hank scoffed. "My situation is nothing like yours."

The man shrugged. "I'm just sayin' if you want her back, try something different."

"He has a point," Adam agreed.

For the remainder of the drive to the station and over the next few days, Hank chewed on that.

28

With sleep deprivation from two insane nights at the station followed by a pair of challenging appliance repair jobs, Hank was all but dead Wednesday evening. Sprawling on the couch in front of the tube, he wolfed down his Chinese-to-go and tuned to ESPN.

He usually enjoyed whatever show was on, but tonight he couldn't have said what the program was to save his soul. His thoughts were elsewhere. On Deanna. He wished she was here keeping him company instead of cursing the day she'd gotten involved with his sorry ass.

As bad as he missed her, he couldn't deny that she was better off without him. For that reason he'd dismissed the baloney Adam and Ethan had fed him. They meant well but didn't know squat about—

Hank's cell buzzed. Hudson. "Yo," he greeted.

"You're still awake," his brother said.

"And fading fast." Hank muted the tube. "How's your partner's leg?"

"Coming along. He sees a couple patients a day now, but I'm still putting in longer hours than I'd like. A week till Thanksgiving and it can't come soon enough. I sure am ready for a whole day off. What are your plans?"

"Max and Daniel are coming over to eat and watch the game." Hank looked forward to that. "You?"

"Going to Mel's mom's place."

"Is that good or bad?"

"She likes me and she's a decent cook, so I'm not complaining. Need to run something by you."

"Shoot."

"I'm thinking about proposing to Mel in a couple weeks."

Hank sat up. "No effing way."

"Believe me, I'm as surprised as you. I never expected to fall in love."

Almost there himself, Hank understood. "Congrats. Can't wait to meet her over the Christmas holidays."

"Save the good wishes until she says yes."

Hank snorted. "Like she'd turn you down."

"It's a concern. She's high-quality goods and could hold out for a better man."

"Are you out of your mind? From the few times Mel and I have talked it's obvious she's wild about you. Hell, you're a partner in a successful veterinary business and one of the best men I know."

"I'm your big brother. You're seriously biased."

"I mean it. Where is this coming from?"

Hudson hesitated. "You don't want to hear my crap."

"Hey, this is me you're talking to—your brother and friend. So yeah, I do."

"Okay, since you asked. I'm fully aware that I don't measure up."

Hank hooted in disbelief. "By whose standards?"

"Dear old Mom and Dad's. Call it a gift that keeps on giving."

"Come on, Hudson, you're the first born, the son they wanted. Your grades, the varsity letter you earned in football, your after-school job at the local vet's—everything you accomplished did them proud. Now, me... I was the unwelcome surprise, the kid who always let them down."

"They traveled so much they didn't have time for either of us. Which is no excuse for them being harder on you than they were on me. It was wrong." Hudson cleared his throat. "I never acknowledged that and I should have. I'm sorry."

As close as Hank was with his brother, Hudson's failure to recognize this had always bothered him. Hearing the words now lifted an invisible weight from his shoulders and made him feel better. "I appreciate that, bro. I don't remember ever pleasing them. The day Cayenne ran away, they wrote me off for good."

"I didn't escape unscathed, either. They jumped down my throat for not watching either of you more closely."

"You knew I was right across the street—you could look out and see me from your bedroom window. Anyway, I'm the dolt who left the door open. I clearly remember Dad reaming me out and Mom shaking her head like I was the biggest disappointment ever."

Fueled by memories and unable to sit still, Hank stacked the empty takeout containers and carried them to the kitchen.

"You were eight years old, just a kid," Hudson said. "Cayenne was always trying to get out. I knew that and I should have checked the door when you left."

"That mistake was mine, not yours. Remember what we did when we realized he'd gotten out?"

"That's not something a guy forgets," Hudson replied. "We tried everything we could think of to find him—put up posters, checked with the pound twice a day, and told everyone, even strangers, to be on the lookout for a red setter answering to the name 'Cayenne.'

"Instead of giving us credit for taking initiative, Mom and Dad kept us in the hot seat. Then they left for Africa. When they came home they never mentioned it again."

Hank looped back to the living room. "That's how they did things—get mad, then sweep whatever happened under the rug without further discussion. Did they even notice how bad we felt? Hell, no. They shut us out."

"More often than not," Hudson agreed. "They were crappy parents who always put their work first."

"And each other." Hank returned to the sofa and plopped down. "All these years I blamed myself for what happened to Cayenne."

"I've carried the same burden."

"Crap, that sucks." Rolling his shoulders, Hank stared at the floor. "How come we never talked about this before?"

"I felt too shitty to bring it up."

"Same here." Hank shook his head. "It's been what—twenty-two years? Better late than never."

"And high time we put the past behind us."

They both went quiet, absorbing the momentous implications of what they'd revealed.

Hudson broke the silence first. "This is going to sound corny, but here goes. I absolve you for any blame associated with Cayenne and for all the other crap Mom and Dad laid on you."

"I deserved some of it, but back at ya on Cayenne.

Man, it feels good to have that out in the open." Hank grinned. "I'd wish you luck with the marriage proposal, but you don't need it. Let me know, and if we don't touch base before Thanksgiving, have a good one."

Not long after they disconnected, Hank crawled into bed. As beat as he was, he was too jazzed to sleep. The conversation with Hudson had cleared away a lot of old baggage and released invisible shackles Hank hadn't realized he wore.

But one biggie remained. Forgiveness. Not for his parents—they were who they were and had done the best they could. For himself. He hadn't let himself off the hook.

Now seemed a good time.

Head propped on his arms, he lay on his back in the dark and sought out the right words. "I make my share of mistakes, but overall I'm a decent guy," he said out loud.

Almost right. He tried again. "I'm a good man."

Nailed it. Hank laughed. Feeling better about himself than he could ever recall, he considered what his new understanding and self-acceptance meant in regard to love.

For years, believing himself unworthy of giving or receiving love, he'd always cut and run from a relationship before his feelings got too deep. He didn't want to do that anymore.

Maybe Deanna wasn't better off without him. Strike the "maybe." They belonged together.

He loved her and had for a while—and wasn't that an eye opener.

He was worth loving in return and was sure he could make her happy. All he needed was the chance to convince her.

Not so easy when she refused to talk to him.

Thanks to Ethan, he knew what to do. It was time to think outside the box.

SHIVERING, Deanna stepped outside to snatch the Monday edition of Guff's Lake News from the stoop. Although the temperature in the area rarely dropped below freezing, this morning felt cold enough to snow. With the thick blanket of clouds covering the sky it could happen.

Lucky she had today off. As she turned to hurry inside, she spotted a package in the large decorative pot the former tenant had left beside the door. Her name was printed on the package in black marker and in Hank's handwriting.

Another one? Catching her breath she picked it up. About half the size of a shoe box, it wasn't at all heavy.

As she brought it into the apartment she fought a smile, then gave in and let it bloom. Hank must have delivered it while she was still asleep. Driving seven or so miles out of his way to drop it off before his shift started seemed like a lot of trouble, but he'd done this before.

The first gift had arrived a few days after the depressing dinner with Vi. A stunning bouquet of autumn crocus, sweet olive, and orange grape, delivered to Deanna at work. Nothing but a single word on the card—Hank. Her colleagues had been so impressed. As had she. He remembered her comment about the flowers Rick had sent Vi—just because.

Then, the day before Thanksgiving, she'd arrived home from work to find a woman's tool belt propped against the door, equipped with a hammer, tape measure, and several sizes of screwdriver. This message was also short—Miss you.

Now, a week and a half later, this.

Gifts following a breakup—another first in her life. For that matter gifts from a man, period. In the past, the guys she'd dated had never thought to give her anything except the occasional meal out.

Deanna shook her head. She had to admit Hank's thoughtful presents had steadily eroded her resolve to forget him and move on.

Unlike the other gifts, this one came wrapped in brown paper. As excited as a child on Christmas morning, she FaceTimed Vi at work. "Look what I found on the porch."

"Ooh, a new surprise. Angie, come see this!"

In the background, Vi's coworker clapped her hands. "How exciting!"

"Hurry and open it, Dee," Vi said. "Prop up the phone so Angie and I can watch."

Deanna tore off the packaging to reveal a plain, white box with no identifying label of any kind. Beyond curious, she tossed the lid aside and peeled back layers of tissue paper. At last she reached the prize. Hardly believing her eyes, she lifted it out. And teared up. "Oh, my gosh—I don't believe this."

"We can't make out what it is," Vi said. " Hold it closer to the screen."

"Remember the ceramic frog Mrs. Steen gave me in eighth grade?"

Vi nodded. "You were so upset when you lost it in the fire."

"Hank bought me a replacement." Deanna held the figure out for her friend and Angie to see.

"Oh, my." Angie laid her hand over her heart. "I've

never met Hank, only seen his picture, and I'm old enough to be his mother, but I'm half in love with him myself."

"Me, too, but don't tell Rick." Vi sighed. "What does this note say?"

Deanna carefully set the frog aside. Then with fingers that trembled she extracted the card from the envelope and read it aloud. 'Can we talk?' "

Sniffling, Vi swiped her eyes. "Please tell me you're going to say yes."

Backing down from a decision wasn't Deanna's style, especially when her pride was involved. Nor was she at all sure she could trust Hank.

"I don't know yet," she said. "But I will think about it."

29

"Hudson's engaged," Hank announced at the station over Monday morning breakfast. His brother had popped the question Saturday night.

"Hard to believe one of the Gardener brothers finally bit the dust," Max said.

Happy for his brother, Hank grinned. "Never would've believed it myself. Hudson is giddy."

"Do you like his woman?" Gus asked.

"From what I know. We've only spoken on the phone, but I'll get to meet her over Christmas." Hank looked forward to that.

"Since the subject has come up..." Rafe set his breakfast sandwich down. "Christmas Eve, I'm proposing to Jillian. She wants a baby and I'm ready to start trying."

"Way to go, man," Adam said. "Just don't tie the knot before Sam and me next spring. She's all excited about our wedding being the first of the bunch."

Everyone chimed in with congratulations before Adam glanced at Hank. "Any word from Deanna?"

Every man in the room knew what Hank had been up to and they all stilled. He shook his head. "Nada."

Neither the flowers nor the tool belt had softened her toward him, but he'd been sure the frog would do the trick. After a full week of continued silence he knew that this gesture, too, had failed. Disappointment weighed heavy in his chest.

Adam slanted him a look. "What's your next move?"

Good question. It had been over five weeks since Deanna had spoken to him, and he felt like he'd been banging his head against a steel wall.

He needed a chance to prove he was a good man, but he wasn't stupid. "If she wanted to be with me, wouldn't I have heard from her by now?"

No one replied, but several of his crewmates shifted in their chairs and muttered, seeming as miserable over the whole thing as he was.

"Sometimes it takes awhile," Gus pointed out. "Wanda and I were separated about as long as you and Deanna have been. Give her a little more time."

"Yeah, but when you went after Wanda, she was willing to listen," Hank reminded him. Not so with Deanna. "I don't want to overdo the gift thing. I'll wait and see what happens."

If he didn't hear from her soon...

He didn't know what he'd do.

FOR THE FIRST time since Hank had started leaving his wonderful after-breakup gifts, Deanna hadn't received one. It had been two whole weeks. She missed them and his notes, brief as they were.

But then, she hadn't thanked him, which was rude.

Maybe he was sick of waiting to hear from her. What if he'd written her off?

Her heart contracted painfully. It seemed so unfair when she hadn't even made up her mind whether to give him a second chance.

While she painted the dining room ceiling at Oliver's Monday morning she wrestled with what to do. Given the ceiling's twenty-foot height and the long-handled roller that didn't quite reach, thinking and painting at the same time wasn't so easy. Neither was balancing on the second-highest rung of the six-foot-tall stepladder.

Having recently sold the plot adjacent to the bed & breakfast for a tidy sum, she could have hired someone. But she wanted to paint the place herself. Besides, she needed most of the money for carpeting, furniture, kitchen appliances, and marketing.

From his place on the windowsill, the ceramic frog, which she'd named Froggy Two, kept her company. He didn't sport a big grin like the original Froggy but his happy expression made her want to laugh. Already she adored him.

Such a sweet, thoughtful gift. That was Hank—generous and considerate. Her heart lifted. As hard as she'd fought to forget him, her feelings hadn't wavered. She was still hopelessly in love with the man.

Not unlike her mother's love for her father. With one huge difference: if Deanna didn't trust Hank she couldn't be with him.

Could she trust him?

That was the billion-dollar question.

"Should I or shouldn't I?" she asked the frog as she bent to add fresh paint to the roller.

Of course, he didn't answer.

"You're no help." Deanna sighed. "I guess it's time I quit wavering and figured out what I want."

She lifted the roller and resumed painting, dripping paint on her cheek in the process. Muttering, she wiped it off with her sleeve. Then stopped.

Who was she kidding? She knew exactly what she wanted—a real relationship with Hank. One where they each felt safe enough to openly and honestly share anything without fear of destroying the bond between them.

She had no idea whether or not that was possible or if he'd thrown in the towel on the whole thing.

She needed to find out.

Right away.

The roller fell from her hands, landing on the drop cloth spread over the floor. Ignoring it, she descended the ladder in record time, wiped her paint-stained hands on her overalls, and hurried through the front door. After locking it, she flew down the front steps, jumped in the car, and hot-footed it to the station.

30

Please don't let him have given up on me. Stomach roiling at the thought, Deanna parked in the visitors' lot adjacent to the fire station. For all she knew, Hank was out fighting a fire or busy with something else, but this was too important to wait.

She'd been so anxious to see him, she hadn't even stopped to grab her parka. By the time she pushed through the front entrance, she was freezing.

The lobby was blissfully warm. And empty except for Deanna and the efficient-looking thirty-something secretary seated behind the glass barrier.

Chafing her arms, Deanna approached the window. The woman gave her an appraising look and the bare minimum of a smile. Deanna didn't understand until she glanced down at herself. No coat, overalls and shirt streaked with paint, her ponytail no doubt a mess... She looked like a freaking nutcase.

"I was painting and forgot my jacket," she explained. Now she sounded crazy, too.

A nod. "Is there something I can help you with?"

Feigning confidence, Deanna smiled. "My name is Deanna Oliver. Is it possible to see Hank?"

The secretary seemed to relax. "So you're Deanna. It's nice to finally put a face with the name. I'm Miranda."

"You've heard about me?"

"Yes. I'm sorry about your house. I'll see if Hank is available." She picked up the phone and made a call, then hung up. "He'll be here shortly. Feel free to look around the lobby."

While Deanna waited she pretended to study the old fire engine in the center of the room. She was too distracted for more than a cursory glance.

By the time Hank stepped through an inner door her nerves were as taught as a tightrope. He strode into the room. Expression guarded, he nodded.

She drank in the sight of him. Dressed in dark blue pants and a white shirt bearing the insignia for the Guff's Lake Fire Department, he looked professional, muscular, and fit. Gorgeous.

Was he pleased to see her? Did he even care anymore? She couldn't tell. Why had she waited all this time to make up her mind?

"Been painting, I see." He pointed at her cheek.

Her face—she'd forgotten. She fingered the dried splotch. "I should've cleaned up and changed clothes before I drove over here."

"What's up?"

He pinned her with his dark gaze. Love for him burned hot inside her, and she forgot everything but her need to straighten things out.

"Hank, I—"

"Hold on." He jerked his chin toward Miranda, who was all eyes. "Deanna and I need a place to talk privately."

"Let me check the schedule." The secretary tapped

several keys on her computer, then gestured behind her. "The first office on the left is available."

"See that we aren't disturbed." Hank led Deanna through the same doorway from which he'd entered, and into the empty office. He shut the door. "I'm on duty. If a call comes through, I'll have to go." She nodded and he went on. "It's been awhile. I didn't expect to see you."

"Well, here I am," she said brightly.

Not even a hint of a smile. He crossed his arms over his chest and rocked back on his heels. "What are you doing here?"

He wasn't making this easy. Deanna hugged her purse. "I gather you're not supposed to have visitors during your work day."

"We get them all the time. I've given my share of impromptu tours. But you're not here for a tour."

"No."

There were two chairs in the room—one at the computer and another next to the desk. He didn't offer her either.

With a sick feeling in her stomach, she knew. He'd changed his mind.

She'd come too far to let that stop her. And she was too nervous to stand. "Can we sit down?" she asked.

Hank motioned her to the chair beside the desk. He took the one on wheels. His eyebrows arched slightly while he waited for her to speak.

"About the gifts..." she started.

A resigned look crossed his face. "Too little or too much?"

"Just right. You didn't give me any old presents. You picked items that are meaningful to me. My first flowers, ever. And the tool belt... You really wowed me with that. Thank you. But Froggy Two—"

"You named the ceramic frog 'Froggy Two'?"

She nodded. "He's adorable, Hank. Perfect. Every gift from you made me feel so special."

"That's what I aimed for. When they made you they threw away the mold. And I mean that in the best way."

He didn't sound like a man who'd changed his mind. Feeling a whole lot better, Deanna released a breath. "You're pretty special yourself."

Instead of brushing off the compliment or reminding her that he was bad news, he flashed a confident smile. "Thanks."

For the first time since they'd entered the office, she really looked at him. "There's something different about you."

"You see that?"

"More sense it. You seem..." She had to stop and search for the right words. "Comfortable in your own skin."

"You always have been perceptive. It's one of the many things I admire about you. I still don't know why you're here."

The make-or-break moment had arrived. Deanna sucked in a breath, the released it. Here goes. "I'm not used to apologizing for my actions, but in this case... That last night with you, I said things I wish I hadn't. I was shocked and I felt so betrayed, I lashed out."

She reached across the desk for his hand and laced her fingers through his. "I accused you of being like all the other men I've known. You're not. You stand head and shoulders above them all."

With an expression of pure relief, Hank raised their twined fingers and kissed the back of her hand. "No apology needed. You had every right to be angry —I lied to you. Hurting you... That hurt me just as bad and I've been paying for it ever since. But some good has come out of the pain."

He let go of her fingers to squeeze the bridge of his nose, and she knew that what he was about to say was difficult for him.

"I've been carrying a shitload of baggage I never knew was there. I'm finally dealing with it and realizing stuff I believed about myself is way off. Sometime I'll tell you about it. Bottom line, I believed I was bad for you and my actions underlined that opinion."

Regret etched lines into the contours of his face, making her ache for him. "I never believed it—until the night I left. I thought you were an amazing guy. I still do."

"You don't know how glad I am to hear that." He picked up her hand again, turned it over, and kissed the sensitive underside of her wrist. "I know now that you and I belong together. Give me a chance to prove it. You won't be sorry."

As ready as she was for that, she first needed to set up boundaries. "I want a relationship, Hank, but not unless we agree to be open and honest. I need to be able to come to you with my fears and concerns, and for you to open up to me. I've never had that kind of trust with a man before, and no matter how deep my feelings are for you, I won't be in a relationship without it."

"Not a problem on my end. If I didn't trust you completely, you wouldn't own my heart."

Trembling, she gazed at him. "Do you mean that?"

"God's honest truth. I'll never keep anything from you again—unless it's a surprise. I—" His eyes filled and his voice cracked. "I love you, Deanna."

Overflowing with joy, she teared up right along

with him. "I love you, too, Hank. I wouldn't admit that if I didn't trust you."

"Fine pair we are, bawling like babies. Come here, you."

She scooted onto his lap and cupped his handsome face in her hands. He nuzzled her nose, then kissed her.

When they pulled apart he shook his head and let out a buoyant laugh. "Hot damn, I feel good." He kissed her again, then drew back. "My brother and his fiancée are coming down for Christmas. I want you to meet them."

"Are you asking me to spend Christmas with you?"

"If you don't have other plans."

"My parents are coming down Christmas Eve and staying at the hotel—my gift to them. Bea will be joining us Christmas Day."

"They're welcome at my place."

"Bea will be so pleased. She's been hoping we'd end up together." Vi was going to flip out. Eyes still damp, Deanna smiled. "I can't think of a better way to spend the holiday. You are so darned sweet."

"Just call me Sugar Man."

They shared another kiss. Things were starting to heat up when the alarm sounded.

"Gotta go." Hank set her on her feet. "We'll finish this Wednesday morning. Expect me as soon as my shift ends."

Deanna beamed at the man she loved. "I'll be waiting."

THE END

THANK you for letting me share my stories with you!

IF YOU ENJOYED **MR. MAY**, help others find this book by recommending it to your friends and by writing a review. If you would like to know when my next release is available and other fun stuff, sign up for my newsletter here: www.annroth.net

THERE ARE 12 sexy firefighter books planned for the **Heroes of Rogue Valley: Calendar Guys**

OTHER BOOKS:
Ann Roth Classics:
Father of the Year
A Place to Belong
My Sisters
Another Life

VISIT ME AT FACEBOOK FACEBOOK.COM/ANNROTHAUTHORPAGE
Follow me on Twitter @Ann_Roth
Email me at ann@annroth.net
Visit my website www.annroth.net

THANKS, and until next time,
Ann

ALSO BY ANN ROTH

Ann Roth Classics

A Place to Belong

Father of the Year

Another Life

My Sisters

Dunlin Shores

Book 1 Just the Way You Are

Book 2 Wedding Bell Blues

Book 3 Falling for Mr. Wrong

Book 4: A Special Kind of Love

Firefighters

Book 1 Mr. January

Book 2 Mr. February

Book 3 Mr. March

Book 4: Mr. April

Book 5: Mr. May

Book 6: Mr. June

Book 7: Mr. July

Book 8: Mr. August

Book 9: Mr. September

Book 10: Mr. December

Halo Island

Book 1 All I Want for Christmas

Book 2 The Pilot's Woman

Book 3 Ooh, Baby!

Book 4 The One I Love

Miracle Falls

Book 1 Christmas in Miracle Falls

Book 2 Dream a Little Dream

Book 3 It Had to Be You

Book 4: You're the One That I Want

Saddlers Prairie

Book 1 Since I Fell for You

Book 2 I'll Be There

Book 3 Until There Was You

ABOUT THE AUTHOR

Ann Roth is an award-winning author of 40-plus contemporary romance and women's fiction novels, as well as novellas and numerous short stories. Her first novel was published in 2000 by Harlequin Special Edition and was nominated by *Romantic Times* as best first book. Ann lives with the love of her life in the Greater Seattle area and enjoys creating flawed characters and putting them in challenging situations that help them grow and ultimately find love— whether or not they're looking for it.

Find out about new releases!
Sign up for my newsletter

Or visit my website www.annroth.net